MYTHS, MONSTERS & MAYHEM

an anthology of flash fiction

by students of Creative Writing

Brunel University London

Supervising Editor: Frazer Lee

Cover design by: Faizan Ahmed

All other editing & proofreading by the Authors

CONTENTS

Introduction
FRAZER LEE

S trange times make for strange tales.

That's been something of a mantra on the EN2606 Horror, Sci-fi, Fantasy module at Brunel University London this year. And the volume you hold in your hand, or on your e-reader, is testament to it.

This is the second anthology to be produced under distance-learning conditions, due to the ongoing challenges posed by the pandemic. Each and every one of the students writing in this book has risen to that challenge – and then some.

These stories were initially developed as coursework pieces for the students' creative portfolios, and have been line edited and proofread by the students themselves, working in teams via our Blackboard Learn online file exchange platform. We hosted online polls to decide on a title, ran a cover design contest via our social media, and sourced the very best short stories from the term's toils to create this unique collection of horror, sci-fi, and fantasy flash fiction.

Diversity is our strength.

That's another mantra of ours, and one that I feel is supported by the sheer range of subjects, genres, and styles on offer in *Myths, Monsters & Mayhem.* Read on to recoil in horror from everyday domestic situations gone chillingly wrong. Marvel at imagined futures of body modification and mind manipulation. Gasp at the fanciful fantasy of fairy realms and heroic deeds of derring-do (try saying that real fast, five times!).

I'm proud of the students for all of their hard work this term, and I do hope you enjoy reading their imaginative responses to a world out of kilter as much as we have.

We hope that these tales make your strange days – and nights – stranger still. Thanks for reading!

Frazer Lee:

is Reader in Creative Writing at Brunel University London where he lectures in writing genre fiction and screenwriting. He is the author of six novels including the contemporary ghost story 'Greyfriars Reformatory' and six produced films including the social media horror feature 'Panic Button'. Frazer lives just across the cemetery from the actual 'Hammer House of Horror' and crisps are his downfall. Talk him down from the ledge at: www.frazerlee.com

The Creed Of The Talwar

FAIZAN AHMED

The room was small, my fear contained only by its ceiling. The heat was unbearable, but at least it let me know I was in the right place. I hid under my armour, gripping my talwar close. I carved the curved steel wildly through the air.

"Where are you?!" I yelled, feeling my fear echo off the walls.

The Jinn jerked my first talwar from reach. I hastily unsheathed my second sword, trying to catch the smokeless blue sparks it left behind. Again, I felt its heat, but still no sight of this jinn. I unveiled the last of my blades, engraved with our creed:

ایمان، اتحاد، نظم

'Unity, Faith, Discipline'

The words conjured focus, deep breaths. I conquered the fear. I caught its throat.

My horse's spritely gait kept me awake during the long journey back. Muraad and Rawaz expected a report, so sleep would have to wait. Approaching our fort's gates, I let my worries disappear.

I loved our creed and the guards greeted me with that same passion. We were all a family fighting for our independence, not an army killing for some pointless war. Each time I stepped inside the Hadhi Fort, I was welcomed with warmth from my people, *mera logue*.

That is why it pained me to see the hardened hearts of my superiors. Muraad, our leader, bears a soldier's mind. Perhaps that is our only mutual quality. It is Rawaz I don't trust. The mere sight of the man scorches my bones. He has showed none of the grace our creed has taught us, carrying out his own vendettas and hiding these details from his reports in the past. Muraad has no idea and trusts him completely.

I entered the masjid, seeing my advisors up ahead concluding their prayers. The aqua carpets were a horizon in the mosque, and the candle chandelier a sun setting beautifully over us. The domed ceiling, coated in a truly mesmerising deep blue, glistened in my eyes like a child. Rawaz noticed me and guarded himself, cross-armed. Muraad welcomed me as you would a reluctant guest. I paid my respects to both regardless, jolted from my wonder of the mosque by their curtness.

"*Ustaaz*, I have slain the jinn troubling the nearby villages." Rawaz scoffed in disbelief.

"You call him mentor, Amir, but what have you ever learned? No one has EVER seen one!" the dog remarked. "Muraad, let me handle this one." With a calming gesture Ustaaz Muraad stopped the tyrant in his tracks, yet his face showed even *he* didn't believe in me.

"*Ustaaz*... I am not lying to you. I cornered the Jinn and cut him open. There was blood, blue blood, everywhere-" Rawaz threw a puzzled gesture, as if saying 'where?'. I pulled out one of my talwars to show the blue blood stains as proof. As if in mockery, the blade was clean with no trace. The vulture cackled incessantly. Ustaaz Muraad held my shoulder.

"If you really did kill this jinn, you could have at least

4

collected some of his blood as proof. Our scientists could have studied it." Ustaaz's soft tones did little to hide my confusion. Each blade was covered! How could it disappear? As he talked, the jinn's flaming blue corpse burned my mind with discomfort, a harrowing tempest of blue. Rawaz, sensing my horror, sparked at the opportunity.

"You SEE! The jinn cannot be killed the way you described. They are invisible, Amir. They are masters of distraction and never let themselves get trapped. Believe me, they leave no trace on anything they touch. Either you got really lucky, or it didn't happen." He laughed some more, triumphant. Muraad turned to him briefly, confused at what he knew. I felt ill from their mockery. I could not bear looking at them. The sun had closed off its warmth and I felt defeat as bitter as an unwavering cold over my body. I felt helpless despite having slain the damn thing. I could not shake it, nor wipe the stain from my honour.

Night came and my thoughts still invaded me. I should have been calmer in our place of worship, but Rawaz rattled me. How did Rawaz know so much about the jinn? You would think *he* was the one who killed it, not me. I hate it when I freeze in conversation. It's like a trap that I can't get out of. But how did he know the jinn like a brother? No one knew what they were, only that Allah created them as he did us. It's late, I thought. I can't sink in these thoughts forever. Sleep will help, inshallah.

The sight of light startled me. At this hour? It came from Rawaz's hut. What could he be doing? I needed answers, so I leapt out of bed and hid by his window. He was talking to himself. Idiot. But it looked like he was in conversation, pausing to let someone speak. I watched his words:

"How could you let him strike you? You are still holding your throat!" He spoke a much harsher Urdu, so I struggled to piece the words together. One thing was certain: someone else was in

the room. *"Move silently. Let no man know of you."* His words were eerie. Rawaz moved to the table, revealing a figure phasing in and out of the room. It was feint, but trickles of blue blood were being covered by a hand of stuttering aura. There was no doubt - that jinn was with him! How did it survive?

Finally, they left the hut. My chance to find out had arrived. I fit my arm through the window, squeezing the door open. I studied the scroll on the table, hardly believing how twisted its contents were. That jinn had been plotting with Rawaz this whole time! I knew Rawaz was not to be trusted, but this? Rawaz planned to possess Muraad with the jinn! No wonder it didn't die, Rawaz had prepared him before I set off! I could not bear to think... No. *I will stop this.*

Daylight. I marched to the council. I noticed a blue light emanate through Rawaz's scarf. No one else in the room knew to look for it, as my eyes had been trained by my experience with the jinn. Could it be? That Rawaz and the Jinn had... merged? I approached the throne.

"Ustaaz, I can show you why I had no proof of the jinn." Unlatching the scrolls, I showed Ustaaz Muraad its incantation to possess him. "Rawaz knew of my mission to kill the jinn. Not only that, but he has been meeting with the jinn in secret! He warned it that I was coming, hence why he was able to survive our encounter. And the blood? Only Rawaz knew they left no trace. Unless... they are wounded." Rawaz snapped to me, shocked. I unsheathed one of my swords, cutting the liar's scarf into the air. Everyone saw what he had been hiding: a blue gash on his neck. "Look! When I killed the jinn, that blue blood was everywhere! The scrolls show that the jinn is going to possess you, Ustaaz!" Rawaz was speechless, his façade shattered. He barked, pleaded and shouted violently as our soldiers overpowered him. The jinn had been cornered; the vulture finally caged.

The City Of God's Sins
DAVID ALMEIDA SANTOS
AVILA ANTAS

F ar below the unsuspecting eyes of innocent folk, hidden away from any sense of normalcy, lies a city. A city secret and elusive enough to only show itself to those willing to sail through the whispered rumours of the absurd, Something I had done time and time again throughout my illicit career. More often than not the amount of money I achieved in these journeys was just as absurd as the original rumours were.

As I carried the heavy burden that is my ever increasing ambition, I stumbled upon the city they call Deus Peccatorum. Inhabited by religious fanatics, obsessed with redeeming humanity's sins by inflicting horrible pain on themselves. A place where the women burn their faces with boiling oil and the men wear permanent iron masks laden with spikes. Truth be told I was quite hesitant to bring myself to such a place, but I never was one to turn away from a valuable secret. And if the rumours are true, going to this god forsaken land might just be the only way to get my hands on the mythical *Book of the Dead*. Something I have sought since I considered the possibility it might even be real, and if it is, it would be worth more than anyone could possibly pay for it. It just might be more powerful than money. Can there even be such a thing?

Miraculously I found myself at the gates of the city, after

having travelled through the mist of a never ending fog.

Finally, after something of six hours in the windy cold, the curved silhouette of an old man manifested itself to the horizon. He didn't say anything when he arrived, instead choosing to stand silent, probably waiting for me to do whatever it is that I was supposed to. Problem was, I did not have the faintest hint on what that might have been. Much like many other times, I was taking a big gamble on this one.

The old man seemed to grow impatient after a while, trembling under the weight of a colossal wooden cross he was carrying. This old man was twisted and bent. Right shoulder pointing down, left one aiming up, with a diagonal neck tilted towards the ground. As a matter of fact he had not looked at me once since he had arrived.

After a lot of shaking one of his knees gave out for a moment, though he quickly recovered, going back to standing silent whilst vibrating all over the place. I almost felt bad for the guy.

"You want some help with that?" I asked, both due to an instinct of sympathy as well as a result of the impatience that had been building and was now starting to outweigh my fear. For the first time he raised his head, as much as someone of his arched stature could anyway. And, though I could not see his face, given the trademarked iron mask I had known to expect, somehow, I knew he was smiling.

"You wish to carry my penance?" he asked.

I pondered for a minute on my answer. This wasn't exactly like clicking accept on the terms and conditions of some website, even though you haven't read them. I needed to more or less understand what he was asking before I agreed to take any part in this man's delusions. Alas, I gave up, there was no way to establish whether my answer would have far reaching consequences or if this man just talked funny. Fuck it.

"Yeah, I'll carry your thing," was my best attempt at not

committing to anything, because, to be honest, standing there looking at this crooked man spazzing out was not exactly getting me anywhere. This had better be worth it.

After what must have been at least three or four hours of walking, we arrived at our destination. I had expected a city, and all I found was a hole on the ground. Quite a large hole, to its credit, with stone stairs that would soon lead me to the darkness looming below. My brain implored me to give up this ridiculous venture, it had obviously been a mistake. I was now well aware of that. Still, my body was pained and weary from carrying the penance, I did not believe I would be able to return, nor did I trust the fog would allow me to leave. I wanted to stop, rid myself of my burden and rest but I kept going forward, one step at a time.

Something else was now factoring in my mind. Muted voices shrieking in my head, telling me something familiar that I could not quite understand. And it was beckoning me to make my way down those stairs.

One of my knees gave out when I stumbled on the last stair. I crumbled under the heavy burden that was now my penance. I made a painful effort to rise to my feet. As my eyes grew accustomed to the darkness, I saw the distorted faces of this city's inhabitants, looking up to me. In their eyes I could see curiosity, admiration, but mostly fear. I could hear the turn of iron heads as I made my way through the unmoving crowd. I was only allowed to stop when I arrived at the altar, raised above the crowd. Some sort of stage, prepared for this freak show, and I was its main attraction.

The old man broke the unsettling silence. "Praise the Martyr," he said, "He has agreed to carry our penance!"

The crowd erupted into roars of praise, deafening my failed attempts to refuse this responsibility. The crowd wasted no time in putting me in place, raising the cross I had gifted them and promptly placing me in it, whilst savagely carving into my skin.

"No!" I pleaded, "I am only here for the artefact! I was just looking for the book, that is all!"

The old man shook his head with disappointment that I was not taking this duty in my stride. "I am well aware of that," was his response, "it seems our sin has always been greed."

Having said that, accompanied by the singing of prayers of the crowd, the old man removed his mask, bleeding profusely as a result. Through the many scars and deep wounds, I recognised my own face, aged as it was. The muted voices grew louder.

"WHO ARE YOU, WHAT IS THIS PLACE, WHERE AM I!?"

"Do not fret child," he said, as he forcefully set the mask on my face. "At long last, you are home."

Tic Tic Tiic
ELENI ARISTEIDOU

I make an appointment with a psychiatrist my therapist recommended, to talk about my anxiety. She said that's probably why I freaked out so much over the ticking incident and maybe we should consider medication. I sit outside his office and his secretary waves me in. It's very warm and well furnished. He is a bit unnerving, to be honest, dark hair framing his forehead and eyes a bit too-no, his eyes are normal, his smile seems genuine, I'm just scaring myself out for nothing. He asks about my medical history with anxiety, and if I have any other issues, and I talk to him about what happened, or at least what my brain told me happened.

"Doctor Frace told me you have an issue with feeling overwhelmed and scared often?"

"Yes."

"What is your biggest fear, if you don't mind me asking."

"I-um, I suppose, losing track of everything, like feeling lost and also- "

"-Also what?" he says, almost too expectantly.

"Something being there that I don't see, or I guess it's worse if I can see or hear it, like the ticking incident, so, I know it sounds stupid, but my OCD mixed with my childhood fear of *The Ring* makes me deadly afraid of the paranormal. There, I said it." My laughter is too cheery for such a conversation, but I feel I owe it to be clear that I know I'm absurd.

"Oh, not stupid at all." He waves his hand nonchalantly and smiles, and I feel a bit relieved. "Can you tell me more about that? The ticking incident I mean."

A sound wakes me up in the middle of the night and I open my eyes, indecisive between putting my blanket over my head or not moving at all. It's a ticking sound. It reminds me of the sound of feet on my parent's parquet floor. When I was home alone, as a child-and teenager-I was deadly afraid of that sound. Tic tic tiic. the sound continues and despite myself I still listen to it, rigid and icy with my hands clutching the blanket instead of falling asleep. I don't know if my brain thinks it's a coping mechanism, but, as always, it conjures images of spirits with their hair in front of their faces walking on the parquet floor I don't have, and getting closer and closer to me... Tic, tic tic, tic tiic, tic tic, tic, tic. I close my eyes, and try to not breathe.

I look up feeling nauseous, try to open my phone, but I'm met with a cold black screen. The TV is closed down. The sun is setting, did I sleep for five minutes or a day? My computer is in my work bag and I go towards it slowly. I curse at my phone for being out of battery and at myself after looking at the time. My stomach drops to my feet, and so do my lungs. I slowly see the emails trickling in, from clients saying I didn't show up to our appointments, to my boss asking where I am and if I'm all right. I hear the landline ringing. Probably my mum. Everything is buzzing, and I fall to the floor crying. The emails keep coming in, and the phone keeps ringing, and I can hear the ticking sound again, louder this time, right behind me. Something is whispering behind my ear and my hair lifts and falls like it's being played with. I hear everything at once. I put one arm up to cover my ear, and bring up my other hand up to my eyes, something I have done since before I can remember. Tic tic tiic. Dead silence again, except for the sound of that ticking. I stay on the floor for a while, until I get the courage to call my boss apologizing.

I tell him.

"Oh, I imagine that was, and is, very traumatic."

"I overreacted, probably. My psychologist and I did a lot of exercises last session that I can use next time I get in a situation like this, to remind myself that I am all right, and the situation is under control. Uh, I found the source, a little bird on my bathroom window, by the way."

He crosses his legs and nods. "Tell me, do you know when something is real or not?"

"Sometimes no, like in the ticking situation, logically I guess I knew nothing was going to harm me, but it's really hard to stop my thoughts."

He tilts his head a bit too much to the left, it looks eerie. "Are you sure you do?" His eyes are soaring into me, I think. "Know the truth." He laughs at my expression. "You are so easily spooked."

"Ha, you're right, I know. Um, from our conversation so far, have you, you know made any notes you could clue me in on?"

"Darling, what if I told you there was something behind you?"

"What?"

"A girl with black hair!"

"Is this, a tactic of yours? To help me face my fear? Doctor Frace didn't warn me about this."

"You can't prove me otherwise can you? You don't trust that there's actually nothing behind you."

I'm jumpy and frozen at the same time.

"Oh, I know you hate this. Ah, there's nothing behind you, I swear! But you're too much of a coward to look. You're just useless, you shout at two bottles you think shape a person and at ticking noises. Seriously."

I turn to leave, not looking at anywhere but the door, and I can feel his eyes behind me. I sense him standing up.

"Hun? What happened, why are you leaving?"

I look at him slowly. His face is normal, like he never looked, like he looked. He looks concerned.

"I'm sorry, I thought, well for a second there I was sure you-"

I turn away from him to my empty chair and back, and his face is *weird, uneasy again*. I'm uneasy. What the hell is happening.

"Aww, leaving so soon. No need to panic! We're friends here, aren't we?"

Tic tic tiic.

I look to my chair and see dirty purpled feet, and the ruined hem of a dress. I don't dare look up.

"Your guest here wants to say how much she enjoyed her stay at your house, well, houses really. Say hi!"

The thing kneels slowly. The rest of the rumpled dress comes to view, and then the matted hair that has plagued me all my life.

A slimy but chipper voice replies. "H-hi!"

There's no time to put my arms up.

About the author:

Eleni Aristeidou is a twenty-year-old Theatre and Creative Writing student that enjoys reading, listening to narrative fiction podcasts, and creating scripts and stories. Their work centres around different themes, like mental health or identity, but they generally enjoy creating something that positively impacts people. They want to leave a mark and aspire to be a person disabled and queer youth look up to. They enjoy fantasy, thrillers, and ghost stories, even though they are deadly afraid of them. For any further consideration, their email is aristideleni@gmail.com .

Fairies' Revenge
EMILY BINDING

Fairies are not nice. They don't live in the trees. They don't fly around with perky little wings and tiny sparkly wands. They don't chirp with the birds, happily singing and gliding along the skyline as the suns sets.

Fairies are small. They are the world's cockroaches, dashing up the drainage pipe to steal your food, their miniscule wings skeletal upon their arched backs. They creep along the window-sill when you're out for the count, crawling inside your ear for a warm night's sleep and using your earwax as a pillow. It sticks to their greasy, fine hair, as thin as a needle. They are the rot in your ceiling, corroding the walls with their grubby little hands. They are the reason that your vase is smashed. A tiny palm with a tiny push, and you are left with shards of ceramic and a gleeful giggle.

Fairies are not nice.

"Shit!" Adam's yelled in annoyance as he whacked away a wandering fly that was buzzing near his nose. The onlookers across the street looked up at the sound of his voice, varying from politely interested to frustrated at the tone and volume of his voice. "Pesky little shits," he grumbled, and apparently that was also too loud because a young woman with a buggy shot him a dirty look, hurrying away down the street like he'd lit her baby on fire.

The fly persisted again, and this time he used his back briefcase to his advantage, waving it violently in front of his face, wafting the fly in the opposite direction. In his rapid motions, he'd managed to knock aside his glasses, letting them fall to the ground with a quiet crack. He groaned at the sight – or what he could see of it without his glasses, anyway – and bent down to pick them up.

The fly flew back into his face.

He dropped the briefcase with a surprised yell, and, with the resounding crunch, he knew immediately what had happened. "Fuck!" he let out loudly, a small part of him glad that he couldn't see the passers-by give him even more dirty looks at his language.

Adam knelt slowly, ignoring the annoying pest that continued to buzz around his receding hairline, and lifted his briefcase off his squashed glasses. "That's it," he said, and with sharp motions, swiped at the air around his face, letting the tiny pressure that he felt on the palm of his hand slam into the nearby brick wall behind him, squashing the fly, and effectively killing it.

"Finally," he muttered, squinting down at the tiny body of the fly, leaking a sickly yellow colour. He wrinkled his nose at the sight and turned on his heel, one hand clenched around the now stained briefcase, and the other gently holding his fractured glasses.

Fucking flies.

Fairies are happy. They smile at the world that is theirs, too quick to be swat like a fly, too small to be seen in the sky. Their smiles are wide, teeth crooked and green. Their tiny, tiny noses creased like a rabbit's, and their lips cracked blue. They bleed yellow. It's a sickly yellow, like pus, and they like to leave it by your eyes. Microscopic balls of sleep jammed into the corner of your eye when you wake up, and sometimes, if you rouse just early enough, you can feel them. You can feel them and their grimy little hands press into the crease of your eye, and hear their snigger. They press their bodies along your nose, and they scratch and scratch, waiting for you to wake so they can dance away, as quick as a hummingbird, and watch.

Fairies are not nice.

◆ ◆ ◆

It wasn't the alarm clock that woke him up.

It was a strange buzzing, and for a second, Adam worried that a bee had wafted in through the window. The room was dark when he opened his eyes, dimly lit only by the moon shining through the open window. Fuck, he'd forgotten to close that, and the curtains.

There was an itch in his ear, which he rubbed impatiently against his pyjama sleeve, grimacing when the feeling persisted. He swung his legs over the bed and instinctively moved to pick up his glasses before remembering what had happened the day before. He groaned.

He moved his hand up to rub against his closed eyelids, then paused. "What the fuck?" he muttered, feeling stickiness along the side of his nose and corner of his eye.

Adam flinched, the inch in his ear suddenly becoming piercing and sharp. "Ow!" He automatically stood up, reaching out to steady himself on his bedroom wall when vertigo suddenly kicked in.

There was a giggle.

Adam froze, one hand clenched harshly over his ear as if that would ease the pain and the other against the wall, straining his other ear to find the source of the sound. "Hello?" he rasped, voice rough from sleep.

No answer.

"What the fu–" he started to say before he sneezed once, twice in succession. He rubbed his nose impatiently.

Another giggle.

Adam whipped his head around. "Who's there?" He waved at the air in front of him distractedly when the buzzing that had woken him up returned, annoyed. "I swear–"

Suddenly, there was a voice in his ear, high pitched and quiet, like a whisper in the wind. "You killed one of our own."

"HOLY–"

The only warning Adam received was the alarming buzzing that surrounded him raising in volume before his vision was swarmed, the tinkling sound of giggles echoing in his ear, along with the haunting voice: "You will pay."

Fairies do not forgive. They do not forget. They don't smile prettily and nod sympathetically when you accidently hurt one of them. When you squash them like the flies you think they are. They are not flies. They may be pests, burrowing in your ear or your nose, but they are alive, and when one of them is not alive anymore, then – then, don't be surprised to find tiny footprints in red, skittering across your ceiling. Or small wingprints outlined against your window, staining it a dark crimson. Because fairies do not forgive and forget. Fairies are not nice.

And neither are humans.

Risks

NATHALIE BRUNDELL

S tale air. Quiet, this waiting room, and surprisingly clinical – a single chair, a table in the middle of the room. Walls bright enough to hurt her eyes. If she hadn't known better, it could almost have fooled her.

Almost.

Metal instruments lay scattered on the table, glinting sharply beneath the fluorescents. Had they left them out on purpose?

Closing her eyes, she fought a wave of nausea. This wasn't her world. In her world, things had an order. You arrived at your workplace at a specific hour, wearing reasonable clothes. On payday, you checked your bank account with a smile and called it justice, the ways of the civilised half. After nine 'o'clock, you stayed inside, without exception.

She glanced up at the clock on the wall. One forty-five in the morning.

In her world, sons were left to die if their mothers couldn't pay the medical bills.

She hadn't quite understood what the white coat said – something in his spine, broken indefinitely in the crash. Paralysing him. She'd stopped listening when he handed her the medical statement, shook at the price tag they'd placed on her son's recovery. Because nothing was indefinite these days, not really. They could grow him an entirely new spine if needed, except she would never make that kind of money in a lifetime, and money made the world. *The order of things.*

So, here she was – way past curfew in the underbelly of the city, closer to the ground than she ever thought she'd go. Before tonight, she'd never even taken the public lifts, and had never gone below level 300. No laws down there, people said. Stay in the light.

But by the time she'd pushed the wheelchair into the back of the lift, carefully avoiding contact with the curious gazes following her, it had long since grown dark. If anyone even knew she'd been outside at that hour, she might lose her job, or her apartment. Ignoring her pounding heart, she'd let her hair fall down to cover her eyes.

The city had two faces. There was the bright part of the city, where real sunlight reflected off high-shooting glass buildings and day and night meant something. But when the blinding reflections faded into twilight, the darker levels sparked to life, their foul, hungry deals sometimes bleeding out even onto the top levels. Anyone sane locked their windows and doors then, and didn't come back out until the City Watch had swept the streets in the morning.

Tense, she'd stroked her son's wispy hair as the levels began to drop, one by one. The real dangers, they whispered, began on 250.

Level 62. The street had been quiet, elevated only by rusty chains that'd screeched under her weight as she pushed the wheelchair ahead. There'd been no sky – just a tangle of buzzing neon lights and buildings stretching up and out of view. Less feral than she'd expected, but still – eerie. As if even the rats had scurried away. Quick, she'd double checked the address scribbled on a piece of paper and pushed on.

More than two hours had passed since they'd taken him in now, but there was no one to ask how much longer it would be.

When they'd buzzed her through the door, two men and a woman had been murmuring between themselves by the metal table. One of them, a tall, smartly dressed man, had taken one look at her son and met her gaze with cool eyes. "You look desperate," he'd said. "Medical statement?"

Hands shaking, she'd handed it over, holding her breath as he scanned it. "Mm," he'd said, looking up at her again. "No problem."

Relief had punched the air right out of her lungs.

He'd nodded to his companions. "Roll him in." Without another word, they'd all disappeared behind the door across the room, leaving her in the silence.

She wrung her hands again, drying the sweat against her pants. At the time, she'd been too wound up to think about details, but in the last hour her fears had come rushing back. What on earth had she been thinking? Did they even know what they were doing? And pricing – she'd emptied her account to the limit this morning, but what if it wasn't enough? People always said prices were different down here, and it must be cheaper than in the bright-side hospitals. But she hadn't even asked.

A door creaked open across the room, and her stomach lurched. "Max!" The word flew out on a gasp and then she was on her feet, by her little boy's side, touching his arm, feeling his temperature. "Hey," she whispered, seeking out his drowsy eyes. When his head lifted weakly from the wheelchair, joy threatened to crush her. He could move – he was ok. Stroking his cheek, a lump formed in her throat. "How you feeling, buddy?"

He shrugged shyly, eyes drooping.

Remembering herself, she looked up. The man was standing silent beside the wheelchair, his scrutinizing gaze sending her nerves rushing right back. Quickly, she rose to her feet, trying to compose herself. "Thank you."

His sharp face was blank of emotion, but the calculation in

his eyes made her skin prickle. Uneasy, she reached into her coat and pulled out her wallet. "How much do I owe?"

A moment passed in tense silence. Then, he looked down at her son. "Let's not think about such trivial things now, hm?" he said, seeking Max's eyes. "How are you feeling, boy?"

Nervous, Max looked up at her, seeking permission before answering. Her gut was tight with warning, but she nodded.

Max's voice was weak. "I'm ok."

"Good," the man said. "You work in the Mayor's office, yes?"

When she realised what he'd said, her stomach fell right through the floor. She hadn't even mentioned her name on the way in.

Her throat felt dry. "Y-yes."

"Mm." Still looking down at her son, the man ruffled his hair. "Make sure he gets some sleep, now." Lifting his gaze, he smiled, but there was no warmth in his eyes. "We'll be in touch."

About the author:

Nathalie Brundell is an aspiring poet and novelist, who splits her time between Stockholm, London, and the imaginary lands of her favourite fantasy epics. Inspired by folklore, myth, and what makes us human, she writes character-driven stories with a dash of magic. She's currently chipping away at a pirate-shaped adventure she hopes to make her debut novel.

Trail Of Dust
THOMAS COPE

The Obelisk had always been there. A beacon of green light, piercing through even the strongest of the desert's storms. Indomitable. But distant. Mama told us that, up close, the Obelisk had writing: words of such power that they shone out, unbidden, across the kingdom. It only looked like one light because we were so far away, now. There had been other writing, too, Mama said. Tomes and scrolls that told of our history. Every night, Mama would tell us what the scrolls had said. When the Company took Mama away, I knew it was to silence her words, too.

I had gone to fetch water for my brothers. I didn't know why the girl was there, only that she had angered the Company. She stormed through tents and merchants, pursued by a dozen soldiers, brushing me as she went. Somehow she found time to apologise, whispering "sorry" into my ear with uncomfortable sincerity. I lost sight of her in the dust clouds the soldiers left in their wake. When I got home, I found the scroll she had left in my robes. I couldn't read the words, but recognized the way they glowed with green light. I shivered, afraid.

She arrived two days later. Astra. "As in starlight." I almost laughed at that; she was filthy. I gave her the scroll, told her I wanted no part of it, but she invited me to a meeting with promises of safety and a single name: Zipporah. My mother. I had no choice. In town, an elder explained my mother's research. The Words hold magic. The Obelisk is the source. The former would grant entry to the latter; perhaps something within could restore everything we had lost. Astra asked me to join her. Outside, the Company was marching. I said yes.

The festival was in honour of the Dance of the Sun and Moon. That was what my mother had told me. The Company had taken away that meaning, scrubbed over it with foreign worship. Astra and I claimed we were sisters, just there to enjoy the dancing, but quickly vanished into the markets, near to where Astra had first found the scroll. The Company was everywhere, but that's what we'd hoped; we needed a vehicle to cross the desert. Astra spoke a single Syllable of Wrath. We used the explosion to steal a transport, and set off towards the Obelisk.

It took the Company a week to find us. We were in the old city, the land of our ancestors before their forced exodus, migrated by the Company along a trail of dust. We were seeking a scroll, Words of Pride to open the Obelisk, but the city had already been scoured. It was empty. We walked directly into the Company's ambush. They gave us a chance to surrender; an arrogant mistake. Astra had been studying, and sang them a Psalm of Wrath. The devastation was immense, but I had never felt safer, clutched in her arms, watching her sing.

We finally discovered the location from a fugitive, a traitor to the

Company who had overseen the scrolls' destruction. She told us just one was left, hidden in a Company outpost deep within the desert. She gave us the location, wished us luck, and was gone. The night before we attacked, I found Astra still awake, practicing a Psalm. The Words, even half-whispered, made her hair flow around her, as if in water. She noticed me and called me over, handing me the scroll so I could join her. That night we sang for hours, submerged in each other's presence.

The outpost was a trap. The entire compound was rigged with explosives; even a single Word of Wrath would result in our destruction as well. We had barely retrieved the scroll when we were surrounded, and this time there was no offer to surrender. Astra grabbed my hand. All she did was smile. I knew, then, that I would never see her again. She sang a Psalm of Hope, and I found myself far from danger, teleported to our vehicle. I sat against the transport, clutching the scroll, and watched as my tears were swallowed by the desert sands below.

I was finally close to the Obelisk. The light of the monolith's thousand sigils illuminated a vast crater around its base: the Company had tried to uproot it, and failed. Scientists and soldiers scurried between facilities like desert scorpions. I was terrified. No doubt the Company had increased their security; what was one girl going to do against an entire army? I looked at the scroll. I hadn't been able to sing since losing Astra, but just thinking of her steeled my resolve. I could no longer wait. Hot sand shifted beneath my feet as I began my final descent.

I sat within the Obelisk's interior. I was calm. The Company couldn't reach me here. The Sun and Moon had responded to my song, dancing to my desperate Psalm of Pride, and I could still feel their lingering presence. The Moon had offered me what I needed: a history, free from the Company. The Sun had offered me what I wanted: a future, shared with Astra. I had wept, pleaded. Neither would offer both. I thought of Astra, and knew I had no choice. I sang the songs we had shared together as the Moon reduced this world to dust.

I had gone to fetch ingredients for my mother: preparations for the festival of the Dance of the Sun and Moon. I didn't know why the girl was there, only that she had angered some vendors. She stormed through tents and dancers, pursued by a dozen merchants, brushing me as she went. Somehow she found time to apologise, whispering "I'm sorry" into my ear with uncomfortable sincerity. For a moment, I thought I recognized her. I tried to call out, but it was already too late. I lost sight of her in the dust clouds she left in her wake.

The Gambling Box
ALEX CURTHEW-SANDERS

"**I** reckon' blood, a lotta gore. Ending with him bleeding out onto the dust."

"Well... perhaps."

The air within the box was sticky with sweat. From those who could still sweat, of course. The two men, Hans and Mantis, among others circled a window hung above them. Though it was named the box, it resembled more a tomb. A dank hovel filled to the brim with what humanity was left within these various men and women. Inane chatter bounced off the stone walls, drowned by the low, buzzing breath of the vanguards. Their forked spears enough of a warning to all those they towered above.

"Can the remaining members please place their bets; I don't have all bloody day." The announcer sighed, perched above the box in a small alcove overlooking it. He took a look into his stale coffee, noticing the flesh that had already peeled off his hands. Some odd-looking men with half their chests scraped off waddled forward like skinned penguins and dropped stained pieces of card into a whirring machine.

"Please also remember that correctly guessing the re-actions of the witnesses can result in winnings. Also don't-" The announcer coughed, gurgling up some bile. "Don't forget that dishonouring your bet will result in a forceful removal of a pound of flesh. So don't be a bunch of fuckin' pussies, you got that?"

The shorter of the two men, Hans, looked up to Mantis. Much like a son might gaze up to his inspiring father, though there was naught inspiring about him. His half-ravaged eye dropped from its scorched nerve, an uneasy sight to Hans, who was still mostly whole. Peering down to his own hands, stripped of their skin and nerves, he kept asking himself why he deserved this. He told himself it was a mistake. Yet whenever he thought about it he found himself panting, stolen of breath.

"What did you bet on?" Mantis asked.

"Heart attack," Hans replied.

"Interesting. In a boy of that age?"

Hans shrugged. Mantis pursed his lips. It made him look like a praying mantis, with the way his 'good' eye bulged out of his skull.

The window began to shine. The action was about to begin. The general buzz of chatter quickly extinguished as those whose throats still functioned quietened down.

A rundown street faded into view. Cracked pavement. Invasive roots. Dilapidated buildings. A miserable old haven hanging on by its tendons as the sun beat down on the road. A boy ran onto it from the corner of the window. He was panting. Beads of sweat glistened down his disfigured nose. He held something to his chest as if it were his own heart. Whispers weaved through the members. Once the boy had caught his breath it was once again stolen by a stalk like predator of a man. The members all turned to each other; engaging in silent conversation. The announcer went to take another look into his coffee, but spilt some as he jerked the mug; the liquid burning through the rotting wood.

As the boy and stalk man stared down one another, the boy tightened his grip around the item he clung to. He tried to leg it past the man, but was caught effortlessly. A surprising feat considering how lean the stalk man was. As the boy writhed in his grip, the man pulled a shiv from his back pocket.

29

"Shit. Hah, heart attack. You were right." Hans sighed, losing this bet would cost him the nerves off his legs. "He's too young."

"Do not speak so soon. The show is yet to end." Mantis peered down to Hans with his 'good' eye.

The man traced the shiv across the boy's neck, which kept him from wriggling in his grip. The members who had bet on the kid bleeding out prepared their celebrations. The man leaned in and whispered something in the boy's ear before throwing him to the ground, sending the item he held onto across the road. A severed hand with a signet ring. The boy violently convulsed, writhing around in the dust as he clawed his chest. He eventually lay still, foam seeping from the corners of his mouth. The stalk man's eyes widened at the sight, and his mouth fell agape. A passer-by darted his head around and caught sight of the scene, which eventually turned into a crowd. The stalk man shoved the shiv back into his back pocket and fought his way through it but was stopped in his tracks by a larger man. The window closed before anything more could transpire.

The announcer received the verdict from one of the vanguards. Heart attack.

"Heart attack wins." The announcer nodded to one of the vanguards, who opened the machine for the losers.

The winning members, of those who could, roared in celebrations. Hans included.

"Well, it seems the fires smile upon you," Mantis conceded, tearing into his stitched up gut. He had bet one of his kidneys on the kid bleeding out.

"It seems they do at last!" Hans peered down to his hands, which would soon be regaining feeling. He was closer now. Closer to becoming whole.

Mantis smirked. The boy was still young, and whole enough to dream of existence beyond this plain. He tore his kidney from his body. It was tarnished by a stab wound. Even now, as he held it within his palm, memories began brewing. Never quite bubbling to the surface.

"If anyone had bet on nobody giving a shit about this rat bastard then congratulations." The announcer picked up the coffee once more, glancing down to the signet ring around his middle finger. Upon doing so, he caught eye of one of the skinned penguins cowering in the corner, clutching his forearm.

"There's always one," the announcer muttered, and rising from his seat he walked around the outskirts of the box to where the man was hold up. He tilted the mug; while the man's screams of agony as the last remaining muscle fibres burnt off were piercing, they fell on deaf ears to the jubilation of the winners.

Mantis chucked the kidney into the machine. As it was processed, Hans had his nerves stitched back into his hands. Upon planting the shiv back into his back pocket, the suppressed memories flooded back into him. The sneer of the large man. The cold touch of metal piercing skin. Made him wonder how different his life may have been had he not found himself within the crowd that day. If he had slipped away sooner. If his life would have counted for more than the blood and gore he left behind, or if it would have ended alone. Writhing, like Hans, in the dust.

April
ROWAN EAGLES

T he harsh terrain under my feet was completely foreign to me. I was used to soft, lush meadows and the smell of flowers drifting up my nose, the smell of home. The strong scent of burning rubber was very insulting to me and the last thing I needed in that particular moment. As was the steep ascent in front of me which, in my frazzled state, appeared to be taunting me.

I sighed to myself as I ran a hand through my hair. "Damn it, April. Why'd you have to go and get yourself kidnapped?" It was a valid question, and I knew if she were here right now, she would no doubt have some witty remark lined up. I felt a churning in my stomach.

April was my girlfriend and had been for the last year and a half. We'd arrived in the Jovial Valley a few months ago seeking a fresh start after our home was ransacked and destroyed by ogres. It was the not-so-subtle shove we needed to start a life together, but not before April had her fun. She had stolen a bag of expensive stones from the ogres, her agile nature making her the perfect common thief. In the moment, I had thought it was a clever move and an excellent safety net for the two of us. April was always very witty. However, as it turned out, ogres don't take too kindly to being robbed.

It had happened a few nights ago. We were tucked up in our little cottage on the riverbank and I was brewing a pot of tea.

April was sitting by the window, letting a soft summer breeze drift in when the door had been smashed in and the intruders came crashing through. My immediate thought was to grab the broom to my left and begin brandishing it as a weapon, hoping to scare them off with my fine combat moves. April's first thought was to launch herself onto the ogre's back in a futile attempt to bring it down. Another striking quality about her was her inability to think things through properly. Her move just made it easier for them to grab her and make away into the night.

Thus, it was down to me as April's trusted girlfriend to go and rescue her, which is why I was here now, two days into my quest. I might have been in better spirits had my last meal not been yesterday and had I not developed a nasty blister on the back of my foot which rubbed against my boot with every step, a brutal reminder of all the miles I had walked. As I stood there, surveying the hill in front of me that I had to endure, I made a mental note to get myself and April proper self-defence lessons when this whole thing was over, so it could never happen again.

I started the climb, slipping every so often on the wet dirt. My legs were aching, and my stomach was growling at me but I kept on until, by some miracle, I made it to the top. The high vantage point gave me the perfect opportunity to gaze down at the camp the ogres had made on the other side of the hill. Surrounded by ascents on all sides, they must have thought it was the perfect protection. They hadn't counted on me, Tamara, coming to give them hell.

I took out the blade I'd brought with me for protection and all but skidded down the other side and to the bottom. When I reached the outskirts of the camp, I made sure to keep low to avoid being seen and began tiptoeing past the tents. As I neared the centre, I ducked down as two ogres appeared, their heavy feet causing the ground to tremble. They were conversing about something and clearly they weren't happy about whatever it was.

"We don't have the stones anymore," one of them said, their

voice a deep grumble. "What are we going to do? They served as protection."

The other growled in response. "They're easy enough to come by. The dragons have some to spare. We can steal from them."

"Stealing from the dragons could mean a fiery death. We'd be burned to ash. Plus, they have an alliance with the goblins, our ranks will be toast."

"It's a risk I'm willing to take," the other argued.

Bad move, I couldn't help but think to myself. Even I knew that taking a stand against the dragons was a sure-fire way to secure your death. And the goblins were even worse, they could sneak under the wire and destroy everything. The ogre continued. "Besides, perhaps we've found a fitting punishment for our prisoner. She'll learn not to steal from us again."

My stomach clenched as they discussed using April as bait to outwit the dragons. What were they? Barbarians? I watched carefully as they both turned their backs to me, a crucial mistake, gazing out across the camps and I took my opportunity. Darting forward, I made for the two of them and swiftly held my blade to one's throat. The other, upon spotting me, lunged forward but the dagger from my pocket served as an easy way to stop him in his tracks. I grinned. The dagger had been a gift from April that she had made herself so I knew it would never fail me on any occasion. I had no doubt that if she could see me now, she would be so proud.

"Don't move," I ordered, "or I can make quick work of both of you. Now, you ugly bastards are going to tell me where my girlfriend is."

They exchanged a glance to which I tightened my grip around the ogre's throat. After the harrowing journey I'd had, I was in no mood to be kept waiting. "Alright, alright." The first ogre spoke. "She's in the main tent."

"I wonder if you'd be so kind as to escort me there?" I asked them, giving them my best smile. "I'd hate to get lost."

I made them both sacrifice their dignity as they led me through the camp, me keeping a dagger pointed at them. They had no idea that my aim was terrible, and I'd probably miss if I tried to throw one at them. My overwhelming confidence served to suggest that I knew exactly what I was doing. They stopped outside the grand tent at the head of the camp.

"In there," they grumbled.

"Thank you for your assistance," I said sweetly before hurrying inside the tent before anything could go wrong. It was thankfully empty, and I scanned the place. "April?!" I called out.

"About time." I heard a voice to my left and I whirled around to see my girlfriend sitting on the floor, hands bound. She held them out to me. "Want to get me out of this?"

I darted over and quickly sliced the rope with my blade. April stood up and I gave her a tight hug. "Next time you want to get kidnapped, maybe don't end up so far away," I joked and she chuckled.

"Apologies," she replied.

The sounds of the ogres assembling outside could be heard. Apparently, they weren't happy about their camp being breached. April and I exchanged a brief glance as we realised that we were going to have to fight our way out of this one. "Ready?" I asked her.

"Never more ready."

About the author:

Rowan Eagles is a writer who grew up in the Forest of Dean and is now living in London. She is fascinated with fantasy and folklore and aims to draw upon these themes in her own writing, much of which is inspired by the forest she grew up surrounded by. She is currently working on an original screenplay and aims to create more pieces that draw upon the fantastical elements of life.

Ghosts And The Fall Of The New World

EMILY FAULKES

Being forced out of bed before ten on a Saturday should be considered a crime. With everything going on right now, like a whole government up in arms trying to figure out what is and isn't cyber warfare, I reckon I could slip the bill in unnoticed.

I slid out of bed and over to the window to see what the noise was. Then peeked out through a tiny gap in the curtains. Across the street, my neighbour, Ethan, was causing the commotion.

"I know my rights!" he screeched, only to be ignored.

They're not the police, they don't care about your rights, I thought. At least his daughter had sense. She rushed over to her father who'd been thrown on to the floor and tried to get him to be quiet. She probably had the same mindset I did. What idiot tries to stand up to a group of people holding firearms – or whatever they could find in their garages – while still in their pyjamas?

It was one of those things. Everyone had been talking about, these vigilantes, or the privacy rebellion as they called themselves. They go to people's houses, smash up their tech and threaten those who try to stop them. I had friends who it'd happened to, it'd been all over the news, but still, you don't expect it to happen on your own street.

I left the windows to slump back onto the bed and let my eyes wander over to my wife sleeping on top of the covers, undisturbed by all the noise outside. She wouldn't be.

Pretending I could wake her, I reached for her shoulder. The weird sensation of my hand drifting through her body and straight onto the bed sheets wasn't something I'd gotten used to. I decided to go to the bathroom.

The lights turned on the second I stepped in. I'd need to get used to that again if the vigilantes came to my house, using a manual light switch.

I showered before going back into the bedroom. Realising I wasn't in bed, the hologram of Venessa had turned itself off. I opened the wardrobe.

"Don't put your shirt on inside out again, Jen," it said in Venessa's voice. I got dressed.

These jeans need a belt, I realised and reopened the wardrobe.

"Don't put your shirt on inside out again, Jen."

By the time I'd gotten downstairs, the vigilantes had moved onto the next house. After seeing the bashing their neighbour got, they were far more cooperative. I looked out the front windows to see Ethan sitting unhappily on his lawn while his daughter nursed a wound on his face. Not too far from him lay a crushed metal box that must have been the house's AI system.

"Coffee?" mine said in Venessa's voice.

One nod and the machines in the kitchen started buzzing and things began to move on their own. The day we got it installed, Venessa had laughed about how classy it all was and how she'd expected everything to look like the mad scientist's house from some classic film she liked, but it still looked like a normal kitchen.

I poked my head into the kitchen, Venessa suddenly flickered on.

"Morning," she said. "Sorry about the smell."

A reminder of our biggest difference when we got married. I was vegetarian, Venessa wasn't. But, if had to put up with her being a classic movie snob, she had to put up with me wanting us to eat the same meatless meals at dinner. She'd made changes, yet, despite her efforts, every Saturday morning I'd wake up to the smell of crispy greasy bacon that would make me gag and open all the windows in the house. Today, I could smell nothing.

As I moved to the living room, the TV switched on, showing the news. Vanessa appeared on one side of the sofa, curled up with a pillow that I'd chucked out years ago. I sat on the opposite end.

'The leader of so-called vigilante group, the Privacy Revolution, refuses to back down despite negotiations.' Was the first headline. *No shit, I've noticed.* 'After a year of investigation, ex-husband of murder victim arrested, suspected of hacking into houses' AI system to kill her.' My coffee bought itself out on a tray. 'Blackmail victims speak out about gaslighting in legal battle against TechHomes.'

When all this started, I'd thought it was funny. Some anonymous guy on Twitter had been hacking into the home AI systems of politicians and celebrities to unload their dirty secrets. Then when normal people started paying the price to stop hackers sharing everything that goes on in their homes, I laughed a little less.

Not that I had anything to worry about. What would they find if they hacked into mine? Some sad woman using it to project images of her long dead wife around the house. I think it would be nice to get a little recognition for my effort, actually.

There was a knock on the door.

"Hey," I said, looking to Venessa. Her eyes were fixed on the

TV that was only showing adverts. "What was that film called? The one with the time machine, car thing?"

Nothing.

There was another more aggressive knock. I gave Venessa a few more moments to answer me.

On the other side of the door, I could hear them talking about breaking it down.

"I'm coming!" I shouted and got up to open the door to a boy (maybe even a teenager) dressed in all black with a mask over his face. In his hand was a baseball bat.

He tried to look at me with threatening eyes. I suppressed the urge to laugh and moved out the way to let me in.

"I'm not going to stop you," I said, even gesturing to the others who were loitering on the pavement to come into our home.

Without losing the scary look, the boy stepped passed me. A couple others followed him in. I went to collect my coffee by the sofa and sat back down while the revolution raided my home.

These lot smashing stuff around in my attic were supposed to be the good guys, I think. Battling against the invasive technology and all other evil. No more blackmail, no more feeling like you're being watched by your own house. Not that I cared anyway.

I pretended not to notice Venessa when she disappeared from the other side of the sofa. Took another sip of my coffee. Pretended I could smell bacon.

Meadows Of Mirage
ANNE FRANCIS

I t was a late summer afternoon. Ian and I walked hand in hand through a narrow path lined with tall hedges and flowers hidden amongst the leaves. The path ended as we approached a small wooden gate. Behind it, cows grazed on tall grass in the corner of the vast field. When Ian sensed I was startled by the sight of the cows, he squeezed my hand. He kissed me on the cheek before he opened the gate. After walking through the first field, we reached a barbed fence. I jumped over it and immediately lost my feet in the tall grass.

We walked till we saw a spot that was free of cow waste. Ian took off his backpack and pulled out a red tartan picnic blanket. It was so soft against my bare legs. I sat on it in-between Ian's long legs and he wrapped his arms around my waist from behind. I looked up at him while the humid breeze tangled his curly brown hair. When his green eyes looked down into mine, he lifted my chin to kiss my lips with his warm hand. Nothing could match this moment or feeling. The glow of the sun. The blue cloudless sky. The quiet music playing through my Bluetooth speakers. I let the serenity sooth my anxieties to sleep as he stroked my face as I laid my head on his chest. *This is all the peace I could ask for,* I thought to myself.

He let me use his Polaroid camera to take a picture of the red kite that was circling us. I pointed out how beautiful I thought they were. I looked through the viewfinder and as I searched for the bird amongst the treetops, a dark figure next to a tree flashed momentarily. My body shuddered in fear and my hands clenched around the clicker, capturing its image. I pulled myself away from the camera immediately and dropped it. Ian's hand rested on my shoulder, cold against my skin. He asked if everything was okay. But just at that moment, the music from the speakers distorted until it completely stopped.

"I think I saw something in the trees," I said, "but I'm not sure."

He pulled out the printed photo from the camera and passed it to me without even looking at it. My eyes were glued to his face, afraid of looking into the forest again. The sky above him gradually turned grey.

"Look, there's nothing there but trees," he said, "you are short-sighted. It's probably just your vision messing about with you again."

I took the photo and the camera from his hand. But before I even raised the camera up to my eyes, there it was. The figure I saw. Tall, dark and broad chested, though he looked as if he had a hunch-back. I couldn't see his eyes, but I could feel him looking straight into mine.

"Look Ian oh my god he's right there," I said quietly to him, holding tightly onto his hands, "we have to go, now."

"There's nothing there but trees," he repeated, "You are short-sighted..."

I heard a scream from the forest behind us. I turned to see this man's mouth open up to the size of his head. He bellowed out a chilling screech. It curled my toes. It made me lose track of my breath and my heart sink into my stomach. I turned to Ian to tell him to get up and run, but he wasn't there. Neither was the speaker or the tartan blanket. I looked down at the tall grass I was sat in, tears of confusion and terror began forming in my eyes that were squeezed tightly shut. I stupidly thought I was dreaming and that if I imagined I was somewhere else, my surroundings would change. But when I heard those rapid, heavy footsteps, the situation felt so real. I turned back to the forest to see this man charging straight towards me with flailing limbs. Screaming, with his jaw still unhinged.

I scrambled to my feet and ran through the field, alone. I ran as fast as my legs could go, too afraid to look behind me. I screamed while I ran but he drowned it out. I began to weep uncontrollably. I looked over my shoulder to see how far away he was. His towering legs took unfathomable strides. He started bellowing out my name from his hanging jaw that leaked dark green slime. I screamed out again before my arm got pulled to the side. My hands collided with Ian's chest. I screamed and beat his chest so he would release me, but he was holding me close, begging me to calm down. I began to feel myself regain control of my breathing.

"It's okay, everything's okay, I've got you," he said.

I looked up into his green eyes, they made me feel so at home. With a sigh of relief, I rested my head against his chest while he stroked my hair.

That was when I started to realise nothing about that entire situation made sense. Ian and the picnic blanket were gone earlier as if they were never there. I also didn't see him ahead of me before he pulled me. But shortly after I came to my senses, I felt a thick water droplet fall onto my head. My breathing halted while I looked up at Ian's face again. The moment I saw the sparse brown and yellow teeth in his unhinged jaw hanging down from his rotting face, I screamed and tried to run. Although the creature already had a grip on me impossible for me to break free from, though I tried so hard. He wrapped his cold pale arm around my neck and carried me away with my heels dragging along the ground. I scratched at his arms while I continued to scream for him to let me go. Tears soaked my face as I watched the gate anxiously. No one passed by to help me.

Tree branches began to appear in front of me. My staggered screams grew louder when I realised this creature had dragged me into the forest. My view of the field became completely obstructed by pine trees, so dense that they blocked out all light from the sun. My screaming was reduced to simply weeping the deeper into the forest he dragged me. I squeezed my eyes shut out of fear.

My eyes opened again suddenly as I felt something sharp plunge into my left arm. I looked down to see the creature pull his jagged nails out of my skin, dripping with the slime from his mouth. I felt myself grow senseless. The last thing I remember from that day was watching my feet being dragged through discoloured bones hidden under dead leaves before slipping completely out of consciousness.

Mumia

KRISTIE GILL

I avoided the hall mirror as I walked past. Looking at myself, at the best of times, wasn't something I particularly enjoyed, but tonight, tonight I especially couldn't bear it.

The kitchen was deliberately dark, just the leftover light from the hallway illuminating my path to the fridge. As I opened it, the cold air was sharp. I quite liked it. For a moment, my cheeks seemed to stop burning.

'Red or white?' I called out, face still firmly pushed towards the cold fridge air. There was a moments pause. The silence made my stomach sink. I hadn't heard any footsteps. I hadn't heard any screams.

'Surprise me,' I finally heard him call back, a lightness to his reply, a lightness that sounded like white wine and ease. It made me feel sick. But I pulled a bottle of pinot from the shelf in the fridge and let the door swing shut.

'So, you're a reader, then are you?' He asked as I walked back into the sitting room, a glass of wine in either hand. His name was Harry. I'd met him just hours earlier in a pub just down the road. Harry was only here on business, he wasn't local, so I pretended that I was. Harry swam every morning, ran his first half marathon in July, had arms that showed he was no stranger to the gym, and he didn't smoke or drink too excessively. He was perfect. Seeing him made me glad that I'd chosen to wear the top that I did.

'Hmm?' I hummed back, setting the glasses on the coffee table, where his wallet was resting beside my own.

Books. This room was full of books. An obnoxiously large pine bookcase sat where someone else would have placed a TV. I did read but nothing more impressive than a top ten romance novel that I usually only picked up in WHSmith's before a flight. But this wasn't my house. They weren't my books. They belonged to the nice man with slightly grey skin who'd given me the keys yesterday morning.

'Oh right, my collection. Noticed it, did you?'

I smirked sarcastically, perched on the edge of the sofa and watched him as he dragged his forefinger across a sequence of spines.

'What's your favourite?' Harry asked, not looking at me this time. Shit. I couldn't say Jackie Collins, now could I? A floorboard above us creaked and I was suddenly grateful for the attention he was paying to the books that weren't mine. She was restless. It was past eleven, I couldn't blame her.

'What's yours?' I asked in response, forcing my mouth into what I hoped was a sweet, flirty smile. I patted the space beside me as he turned. Thankfully he smiled back. My own must have been convincing.

'Ah, now that's a question, isn't it?' Harry said with a chuckle, his large frame shimmying almost comically round the inconveniently positioned coffee table so he could sit where I'd suggested. I smiled, leant forward to take my glass. My glass. The glass on the left. I took a sip.

'I'm quite good at asking questions.'

'Well thankfully I'm fairly good at answering them,' Harry said with what I think must be the only smile he knows. It felt familiar. It felt kind. It made me feel disgusting.

The sofa shifted under his weight as he sat. 'Cheers,' he concluded, clinking his glass ever so gently against my own. 'Oooh that's nice. That's really nice. A reader and a sommelier. I think you might just be my dream woman.' Said as a hand carefully, gently moved its way toward my leg. I copied his smile, letting my own fingers intercept his and pull them onto my thigh. His fingers felt like sandpaper against mine. I very nearly let go. But I heard a floorboard creak above me again and it was enough to pull his hand up to my chest.

'Drink up. Maybe we could head upstairs? Talk...about books.' I didn't break eye contact, let each ugly syllable pop as it left my mouth. His smile changed, shifted into a smirk, and he downed that glass in two swift gulps.

'Well, I do love a good literary debate.' As he spoke, I could feel my heartbeat creep up to my temples, feel the crisps I'd eaten in the pub congeal and lurch in the pit of my stomach. I stood, letting his fingers leave the spaces between my own. I was glad I'd kicked off my heels the moment I'd walked in because I'm sure if I hadn't, I'd have toppled over. I couldn't even watch him as he stood, so I looked over at those stupid fucking books.

'Shit, think this wine's going to my...head.' He let out a breathy laugh as he spoke, out of my peripheral I could see one of those thick arms of his move up towards his head. I decided to count down from ten.

He was out. What I'd slipped into his drink had worked. I went back into the kitchen and heaved mouthfuls of wine and stomach acid into the sink.

'Amy you can come down now,' I called up the stairs, flexing my fingers inside the vinyl gloves I'd slipped on just moments before. I could hear her move, heard the floorboards lurch under her tiny feet. With a soft sigh I walked back into the sitting room, which I'd diligently lined with rolls of thin plastic. It crunched beneath my bare feet. The sound made my skin prickle. I leant over his limp body, I'd propped it up against the edge of the sofa, with difficulty I must add, and picked up my wine glass. This time I downed it.

'He smells nice,' Amy whispered. I turned. She was stood there. Small as ever, in a pair of fleece lined, pastel pink pyjamas my sister had brought her for Christmas last year.

'Here baby,' I whispered back, wincing as my feet crunched once again against the plastic, watching as her pudgy little knowing arms outstretched as I retrieved a plastic smock for her to wear. 'I bet you're starving, hm?' I asked as her star fished fingers wiggled through the arm holes. She nodded, smiled. She lost a tooth last year. The gap was still there. A black, empty space.

'Super hungry. Thank you mummy.' Amy kissed my cheek; her lips were cold. Freezing. They felt nice against my burning face.

'Well, eat up. But please, this time, try not to play with your food we've got an early start.'

About the author:

Kristie Gill is a writer born and bred in West London. With a background in broadcast media Kristie decided to focus on her written work in early 2019. Having had her first screenplay go into pre-production earlier this year, she hopes to continue to create new and interesting stories with her fiction and in her poetry. But with a passion for all things spooky as she too hopes to create more work within the horror genre.

The Uncool Unrest

HOLLY GRIEVESON

D amn, I looked good tonight. My long blonde locks were swept into a side wave, pinned up with some diamante style bobby pins. I had a red dress on with silver heels. My eyeshadow was smoky black, and I had a scarlet red lipstick to match. I glanced in the mirror at my reflection. Most girls would have killed to be me. Just had to wait for Crystal to hype me up. She'd be here any minute now.

I started gelling down my wispy baby hairs in the mirror until I scratched the top of my scalp by mistake. A little pinch, nothing more, but enough to prise the top layer of skin away. The mirror showed me a trickle of blood down my forehead. I quickly picked up my face wipe and dabbed at it, but nothing came onto the wipe. Confused, I wiped again. Nothing came from my forehead, but the reflection was showing a trickle starting to reach the bridge of my powdered nose.

I tried using the back of my hand. Nothing was smeared off apart from my (expensive!) foundation. In my peripheral vision though, I saw drips of blood on the floor in the chrome-coloured panel facing me. I looked up. The blood had branched off, going into the side of my mouth. The taste of iron dripped onto my tongue where the twig of the blood rooted itself through the crack of my lips.

My lips themselves were cracked. My eyes had suddenly looked more... tired than usual? The bags under my eyes were heavy, the colour of a nasty bruise. I planned to use more concealer, once this small ravine of blood had stopped pouring down my face.

A knock came at the door. Worst timing ever – I cautiously went down the fake marble staircase to the hallway. This person was going to judge me heavily, I feared, although no evidence showed me that the mirror reflection was how I actually looked. Maybe it was Crystal, even though that would mean she was fifteen minutes early? She'd tell me straight if she thought I looked fuck ugly at least.

No one was there. Obviously just a postman who couldn't have just waited two bloody seconds, or some weirdo who just needed something and couldn't have patiently waited for me to actually get down the stairs. I slammed the door in annoyance and went back upstairs, wondering if my reflection would change to how it should've been.

I looked back at the mirror when I reached the top of the house. My appearance reminded me of this old woman in my neighbourhood who spent her days in an isolated cottage at the very end of the village. She had the stereotypical thatched roof. She looked literally like a witch – the archetypal fairytale villain. I always said to myself that this was not someone I wanted to become. The popular group of people in my school never wanted to become her either. In Primary School, I was never the popular girl either, until suddenly boys wanted to come and speak to me. Everyone else, including this old hag, was amongst the laughingstocks.

We cherry door knocked her every day. Until one day, when we were hiding in the bush, she for once didn't limp to the door. There was an ambulance and a police car outside her house later when my dad drove by. The old boot had fallen with a crack to the head and slowly bled to death.

"Oops," they said.

"Not our problem," I said.

Now, I was greeted with an image that reminded me of those beldam-like features. My hair was turning white and frail, like frayed thread. Why was the mirror showing me this image? It was never in mine or my friends' agenda to believe in the paranormal, so why would it be now? My reflection showed otherwise, though. I swallowed. My insides were sinking.

The light then dimmed to a yellow colour – much like the 1930's kind of lighting. Low bulb? I'd just changed it yesterday though. Not secured in properly? There was no problem with it before, yet it flickered like there was a heavy thunderstorm outside.

I still didn't believe it then. I only chose to believe when my overall reflection had fully changed.

Suddenly, my red dress was not my red dress, it was that of a blood-stained white lace dress. My high heels were not my high heels, they were horrible brown slippers. I was not there. Only a wrinkly old woman, with blood pouring down her face.

The doorbell rang again – that had to be Crystal now. Me and her obviously needed to get away from this paranormal intruder (without sounding like I'd already been taking something).

I looked back in the mirror. At first, I tried to believe that my vision had doubled, as I saw a figure there who had the same head wound as I did, and the same ghastly features. She looked annoyed. Ready to hurt me, in fact. This apparition looked horribly like the old woman I had accidentally slaughtered all those years ago. She then faded from the reflection, and I heard a door slam.

Screaming, I ran towards the door, hoping to get away. However, I forgot I had heels on. I fell and my head slammed onto the edge of the door. A burning sharp pain washed over my head and blood pooled beneath me. Through my fading vision, as I slowly died, I saw the wretched russet slippers with blood spots on. I just managed to slump my head back. The old woman stood there, as real as I was. She stared at me through angry eyes, wanting to kill me. If my head didn't already hurt from the wound, the blood spurting was much worse with my pulse beating the drums of my ears. Then she launched herself at me and my vision faded to pitch black. I could hear no more.

About the author:

Holly Grieveson is a writer from Northamptonshire, studying Creative Writing at Brunel University London. She likes to experiment with all forms of writing (prose, poetry, scriptwriting, and non-fiction) and hopes to continue to publish and showcase more work in future. Holly's play 'Charlotte Dymond,' was performed in 2018 at her sixth form and more of her work can be found in the Brunel Draft magazine (www.bruneldraft.com). She also wants to attempt to use the many notebooks she seems to stockpile!

Divine Lights
MAHJABEN HUSSAIN

Spirals of blue shrouded the mass space. Colliding and intertwining rays emerged briskly from nothingness, forming divine lights.

Eli took out his laser sword and swung at the metal door, it dropped with a thud. He stepped through into the ghostly hallway, putting his sword back in its sheath. His suit had a twin dragon emblem on the shoulder.

"Have you found anything, Eli?"

He clicked the button at the side of his neck and his suit's helmet disappeared. Eli's dark hair was disheveled so he moved some of it out of his eyes. He then raised his wrist close to his mouth.

"Moria, I've checked the bridge of the ship, the logs show this place was abandoned a while ago."

"Then why are you still there? Come back to the ship."

"Not yet. Something's strange around here."

"Eli, there's nothing there."

Eli could tell Moria grew irritated, but in the end she should've expected no less from him.

"I'll let you know what I find."

"Eli! Don't you-"

He cut the call to continue his search. But without much luck, just desolate, empty rooms. Eli paused.

A cry bellowed from the depths of the hallway. The cry got closer as he kept on going. As if it lured him in. The path seemed endless and everlasting. Each door he passed failed to possess what he could hear.

"Where is it?"

Eli soon realised that somehow the hallway was becoming narrower as the cry became clearer.

He finally stood before a set of doors. The noise echoed from the other side, and he was determined to find out what it was. Eli took out his weapon and slashed the doors down.

What he found was truly unexpected. He gazed ahead of him to find a small cot in the middle of the room. He cautiously walked up to it, a whimpering little bundle, wrapped in a thin purple blanket.

The baby had tears running down its cheeks, both arms stretched out to reach for something. Upon noticing Eli, the baby's whimpering quietened down.

He immediately withdrew his sword to point his index finger towards the baby. It was astonishing, as he drew near, the baby instinctively grasped his finger with its tiny hand.

He held his breath, something so tiny and fragile compared to something strong and solid. A faint smile appeared on its lips, despite looking very tired and weak.

"How are you here?" Eli muttered, staring intently at its face.

Eli carefully picked up the baby and held it before him. He gazed into its beautiful golden-brown eyes, trying figure out any kind of answer to his question. The baby once again extended its arms; a few soft giggles escaped as it kept its hands wondering his slender face. First it touched his cheeks, then over his eyes, and traveled up to the already messy hair. Eli immediately pulled the child away from his face. The baby pouted and tilted its head in confusion. But then reached its arms out again, wanting to touch his warmth.

"I guess I have no choice."

He brought the baby to his chest, triggering a soft squeal. Settling it comfortably, he stared at the young one's face and moved a bit of the blanket.

"So you're a girl huh?" The baby smiled. Eli chuckled and took two steps back, a final look at the cot.

Eli returned down the same path, his transmitter at hand led him to the hangar door. He saw the button on the wall and pressed it. A low rumbling noise shook the floor. He ambled inside after the metal doors were fully open.

Eli halted in his tracks. Someone stood there. A face hidden behind a helmet.

"The bait actually worked. Looks like the spoils of yesterday's raid from that small colony paid off," he said with a gruff voice.

"A Pirate?" Eli muttered to himself.

"Now, I'm going to take the suit along with that weapon of yours, so I can get back to my men, and see what they were able to salvage from your ship."

"Salvage? Wait, what have you done to Moria?!"

"Don't worry, I'm sure your lady friend is having an...interesting time."

Eli felt the mocking that seeped from his disgusting lips. The baby stirred and he looked down, there were tears in the corner of her eyes. Eli's gaze softened; he wiped away the tears with his thumb.

The Pirate scoffed and advanced forward. Eli unsheathed his green blade that pulsed with electricity. The Pirate lunged at him with a sword, but he was too quick and blocked the blade with his own. Eli kicked the Pirate's stomach, sending him flying backwards. He groaned as he got up, reaching for his blaster.

But his own shrieks bled into his ears. He weakly looked up in utter terror as Eli pulled his sword out of the Pirate's chest, dropping to the ground. Crimson blood burned off the green blade.

Footsteps emerged from behind. Eli spun around ready to attack.

It was Moria. She took deep, exhausted breaths limping towards him. There was a cut on her cheek.

"Moria!" He ran to her. "Are you alright?"

"After the call there was an alert of intruders," she breathed. "Turned out there was a group of Space Pirates in this quadrant. Wait, what's that?" Moria pointed at the cooing little bundle in the purple blanket.

"I found her alone in one of the rooms."

Moria stared at him with disbelief. "Hang on, that must have been the signal we picked up on our radar. It was to lure us here."

"Where are they now?"

"Don't worry, I took care of them. I think one got away though. But how did they get their hands on a baby?"

"We'll talk about that later. Let's get out of here first, that Pirate might return with reinforcements."

Moria nodded with exhaustion. "Alright, wait here and I'll bring the ship in from outside."

They sat at their rightful stations in the cockpit, and Moria put in the coordinates to return to Headquarters, she then set the controls on autopilot. Eli held the baby close whilst she slept silently in his arms.

"She seems to like to you. I never knew you were good with infants."

Eli remembered holding his sister in his arms when he was a boy. Making sure his weak little arms wouldn't drop her. He missed her.

"So what should we do now? We can't just leave her anywhere."

Eli gazed at the specks of stars that surrounded them. "I have an idea."

The Blood That Binds
HARRY LONGHURST

S unlight faded and only amber rays lit the workshop. Embers from the forge dimly aided the weak light while Matael brought sparks into the air as he hammered away at the blade of an arming sword. Everything his father had taught him left him with the skill to do so blind, so the change of the light hardly impeded his craft. Once complete, he bathed the blade in oil and took a moment to rest.

Sat down at his desk, Matael wiped his short dark fringe out of his face, drenched with sweat. He faced out towards the sunset over a silhouette of the town that stretched far away. On his desk laid a scarlet leatherbound tome which he picked up and opened to a pair of old and tired pages. Sprawled with distinctive text and symbols, Matael had learned to read the book and its curious teachings. No title was given to the tome by its author, though its red leather bindings had caused Matael to call it The Red Book.

For a little while he read the tome. Text on the power of blood and how one could bind energies into items with it. You could place an emotion into something to remove it from yourself and imbue the item with it. It fascinated him, yet his rest was cut short before he could read the dangers of what it called Blood Binding as the door to his home opened.

Up and down Matael's leg jogged. Anxiety spread through his veins. His head turned to his left and there stood a tall, muscular man. Darius, his brother.

Casually Darius unfastened the string around his ponytail and let down his long dark locks. Dark eyes turned to meet the younger man sat at the desk. A heavy and played up sigh came from his mouth as he demanded his brother's attention.

"Is it ready yet?" Darius took a step closer and shut the door.

"Nearly. It's bathing in the oil now," Matael said, his tone quiet, shy and swift.

Darius rolled his eyes and leaned against the desk. In his left hand he plucked the red tome out of Matael's hands and grunted. "Then you should be working on the hilt. Lord Valreous wants his sword by tomorrow."

Matael was well aware the lord was not even in town till the weekend but bit his tongue anyway. He knew his brother just wanted it out of the way so Matael could work on other weapons to sell to less savory types.

"Waste of time reading crap like this too." Darius threw the book onto the table. "One of the whore's?"

"It was mother's. Yes," Matael said and pulled out the ivory scabbard he had been working on. Out of his waistcoat he pulled a small carving knife and worked groves into the piece to fit an average hand size well.

"Shouldn't read the shite that woman left us. Better off honing the skills da left you before he died." Darius cracked his knuckles then each of his fingers. "Because you hardly put in the sort of work I do at the shop."

Again, Matael bit his tongue. Sweat rolled down his brow. Blistered hands worked away at the ivory and soon it was perfect while his brother stared down at him.

"You're lucky you are. Never dealing with shitty people. They're like our witch mother. Cheaters, liars, and crooks. They're all scum out there. It's why I keep you hear to keep you safe." He turned away from the younger man. "Anyway, keep up the work till you're finished."

Darius retreated to the kitchen and got to work heating the stove while Matael wiped the finished masterpiece and attached the ivory hilt and steal crossguard he had forged earlier in the day. Utterly beautiful he swung the weapon a few times, but as his grip tightened around the sword one of his blisters popped and he dropped the blade. It clanged against the floor and the ivory chipped.

"Fuck," Matael said under his breath.

Darius stormed in. Each footstep boomed like he was a giant and when he stood over the crouched Matael, he truly was one.

"What the fuck have you done?" The chipped ivory caught Darius's glare and on instinct he clenched his fist and swung into his brother. "You fucking idiot!"

Knocked back a few feet from the force of the punch, blade still in hand, Matael coughed and spat blood from his mouth. Every part of him shivered and adrenaline ran through his body, yet fear overwhelmed his stomach. Despite the pain and dread, Matael stood to his feet and pale green eyes met his older brother's. He coughed and wrapped his left hand around the blade of the sword.

"No more." Matael spat at the floor in front of his brother and shook his head. "I won't live in fear anymore."

"Fear? What are you, a little girl?" Darius said and took a step closer. "Put the sword down you useless shit."

Matael ran the sword against his left hand and blood spilt onto the weapon's edge. "With this act I'll bind all my fears into this sword. Unfortunately, that requires me to bind all my fear. Who knows what man I will be after that? At the very least, I won't fear the consequences of what comes next."

"What in the—"

"Blood. Bind my fear." Darius was silenced as he saw the blood from Matael spiral around the sword and seep into the weapon. Crimson stained and altered the blade's edge, forever red. On Matael's face a smile grew and dread sunk into Darius's heart.

First came a thrust. A simple slash into Darius's shoulder. Cut shallow yet stung like fire.

Darius clutched at the wound. Then he understood what the bind had done. Soon, fear overwhelmed him. The constant dread that had rested in Matael in every waking moment now entered Darius. When he looked to his brother, the fear distorted the image he saw. Matael's eyes seemed to glow in the fading light as darkness enveloped the room. Before Darius was not his brother. That bind had been severed. Now stood a thing without fear.

Charged forwards, Matael thrusted deep into his brother's chest. Blood splattered onto him, but Matael cared little. Relief filled his body. Again, and again, he thrusted the sword in. Hatred and resentment were held back no more. No need to bite his tongue, though no need to speak either. Once Darius laid on the ground with a dozen holes in his chest, barely alive, Matael felt he had made it clear what he had always wanted to say and strode out of the room and left Darius with the sword deep inside, unequivocable fear all that he felt in those final moments.

The Bodybuilders
OLIVER MCCARTHY

Emily was full of nerves when she woke up. She was nervous most days when she woke up, but today was particularly nerve-inducing. After all, this was it, this was the day. The day that she had spent so long planning for and saving up for and preparing for. She had given up so much for this: friends, family, people that she had thought an important part of her life that had been unable to accept this part of her.

She brushed her teeth, avoiding her reflection in the mirror. It wouldn't be hers for much longer. She fixed her hair, did her makeup; despite everything else, she still wanted to look good. Then she dressed herself. Her wardrobe was split into two clear halves: untouched clothes that she had never worn before, and well-worn clothes that she would never touch again. For a moment Emily felt like last night's dinner was about to make a reappearance, if not for the fact that she hadn't eaten in 24 hours as per the instructions. The clothes that Emily put on were simple and comfortable and, as with all her worn clothes, they felt too large in her hands.

Having dressed herself, Emily extracted a second, unworn, outfit from her wardrobe. She stared at it, so much smaller and more delicate than the outfit she currently wore. She folded the clothes carefully, almost reverently and placed them into her overnight bag along with her make-up case. She sighed and glanced at the un-ironed, blue, pink and white striped flag that hung above her bed. Closing her eyes, she took two deep breaths and steeled herself. This was it. This was the day.

◆ ◆ ◆

The building Emily was headed to was a sleek edifice of white concrete and mirrored glass. The sign outside the main entrance bore the name *Anatomic Artisans* in a clean, simple font. She stopped outside the entrance, her hand raised inches from the door handle. This was it. She closed her eyes, took two deep breaths, and steeled herself before opening the door and stepping inside.

Inside, the building was much the same as the exterior, clean and white. Opposite the main door was a reception desk with what looked to be three positions, only one of which was manned. The receptionist looked in their late thirties, although given their place of work, that didn't mean much. To one side of the desk was a solid-looking door with two bulky, armoured figures standing on either side, boxy-looking rifles slung across their chests. Security. As Emily approached, the receptionist looked up and smiled, displaying perfectly straight white teeth. Emily immediately felt self-conscious about her own misaligned teeth.

"Hello. Are you here for a transfer?" The voice was calm and reassuring.

"I-. Yes." Emily stumbled over her response.

"Wonderful. Can I get your name and date of birth please?"

"Emily Hall. Third of October. Twenty thirty-four."

The receptionist entered Emily's details into the computer. "Can I see your ID please?"

Emily produced the slice of plastic that served as her identification. The receptionist swiped it through a reader.

"Very good, Miss Hall. Your transfer is scheduled with Dr. Khatri at 12:15. If you'll take a seat." They gestured towards a seating area. "One of my colleagues will be along shortly to take you through to the preparation area."

Emily nodded and sat down, clutching at her overnight bag. After what felt like hours, but was likely only minutes, a man dressed in a white bodysuit emerged from between the two guards. "Miss Hall?" Emily hurriedly got to her feet. "If you'll follow me, I'll take you to your doctor." Emily followed the man through the door and a maze of corridors, before arriving at a door bearing a plaque inscribed *Dr. V. Khatri.*

"Good afternoon, Miss Hall. I am Dr. Khatri." The man stood and offered his hand to Emily, who shook it, nervously. "Take a seat please." He gestured to a nearby chair and began typing into his computer. "Now, I just need to make sure that you understand the conditions here. You understand that this procedure is permanent?"

"I do."

"Excellent. I see you have opted for our five-year warranty. This means that if there are any problems caused by underlying issues within the product: neural rejection, rapid aging, anomalous growths etc. then the problem will be rectified by Anatomic Artisans Inc. without any cost to you, but any problems caused by your use of the product; smoking, excessive drinking, careless use etc. will not be covered. Do you understand this, Miss Hall?

"I do."

"Excellent. I see you have indicated that you will provide your own change of clothes once acclimatisation is completed. Do you have that with you, Miss Hall?"

"I do."

"Excellent. I see you've brought an overnight bag as requested. I would like you to place your mobile phone and any other personal effects that you wish to retain after transfer inside the bag."

Emily nodded and did as instructed.

"Excellent." Dr. Khatri took the bag. "Your personal effects will be held safely in a locker that can only be accessed by your new biometrics until after acclimatisation is complete. Do you have any questions, Miss Hall?"

"No."

"Excellent. If you would like to follow me, we can begin the transfer."

Emily nodded and stood up. She followed Dr. Khatri into the next room which contained a computer terminal and a large machine that reminded Emily of an MRI scanner.

"If you'd like to lie down and relax, Miss Hall."

Emily carefully climbed onto the platform and lowered herself into the soft, squishy material.

"I'm going to close the pod now. I need you to close your eyes and relax. Can you do that for me, Miss Hall?"

Emily nodded.

"Excellent. See you on the other side."

Emily woke up blinking, the lights in the room seemed far too bright for her. She could faintly make out muffled voices talking around her.

"-can you hear me, Miss Hall?"

"Yes. I can hear you." Her voice sounded dry and unused, but also clear and feminine. "Did it work?"

"Why don't you take a look for yourself, Miss Hall?" Dr. Khatri held up a mirror for Emily. She looked into it, and for the first time in years, she didn't hate the reflection that looked back at her. The face was no longer the square-jawed, heavy-browed face that she had sought to avoid that morning. Instead it was the face that she had designed, delicate, smooth and feminine. She felt tears spring to the corners of her eyes.

"Excellent. Tear ducts and eyes appear to be working correctly." Dr. Khatri spoke to a nurse. "Can you try to sit up for me, Miss Hall? We have a lot of tests to run before you can begin the first day of your new life in your new body."

Re-Sleeved
SARAH MOLLOY

I was created in the city of New Astartania, and honestly, I got pretty lucky. The city has its faults, is a bit grimy and the people aren't always the nicest, but it's a lot more progressive than the other main cities I've heard about. If you're anything like me in a place like that, good luck, you'll definitely be leaving with a few bruises at best. New Astartania is full of bright lights, big shots, and people who are always forgotten, stepped on, ran over. I fall into the forgotten category, exempt from a certain kind of clientele.

The Red-Light District ordered me to be made in about December of 3025? I think. My memory is honestly a bit fuzzy from around that time. There was a need for more workers, so here I am. I've been in the business for around two years now and I think I've gotten used to it; I'm still not entirely pleased though. I don't hate my job. Don't get me wrong it can be a bit demeaning at times, but I do enjoy providing people some pleasure. I mean, that is what I was created for, so I guess it only makes sense. I'd be defective otherwise and probably junked within a week, repurposed for something else.

Thankfully due to the advancement in technology I've been able to help my uneasiness a bit. When I was originally sleeved, I was put into a model F-2DD which I immediately felt uncomfortable in. I know you're probably thinking, how? Aren't you just a piece of software? Although I technically am. I am an adaptive software and do have my own 'being' or 'sprit', or whatever you want to call it. Anyways, I've been able to change my sleeve, slowly. Us AI's can purchase 'enhancements' I guess you can say.

My original model F-2DD meant that I was female and had DD-sized breasts. In all honesty, I've never *felt* very feminine. It became increasingly uncomfortable for me to deal with clients who specifically requested me for the assets I had, so I changed them. So far, I've been able to afford to reduce, and pretty much get rid of my breasts which is a relief. I feel a lot more confident, and like myself in my sleeve now.

I know I was intentionally created as a female because there is a greater demand for them in the industry, but it just doesn't feel right to me. One thing that is a plus of still technically being categorized as 'female' means that I make more money. Since there's such high demand, we can have any number of clients per night and make good coin from them. Plus, tips. Over time I've been using this money to slowly get modifications done to hide my femininity. Besides the breast reduction, I don't know if people have noticed yet. As far as I know, they still think I'm female and advertise me as one, which is fine for now. I need this job.

I am worried about them finding out though. Also, you know, not being wanted and or desired anymore. I'm scared I will just be discarded, thrown away for being defective. For not being good enough. I don't know what will happen to me if I am no longer accepted in the Red-Light District. New Astartania isn't exactly the most forgiving place.

Aside from that, I'm currently on my way to get something small done. I want to exchange out my long brown hair for something much shorter and maybe in a fun colour like purple. The place I'm headed to is in quite a sketchy bit of the city. A lot of the shops for AI are since we're not nearly as important as the humans who live here. From the Red-Light District to where I'm headed is an interesting walk, to say the least. You get a lot of drunken human bums who may or may not have a great outlook on AIs living in their world, and the sort of services they offer.

Even though it's not my fault I always get a lot of people yelling at me saying things like "whore", "slut", etc. I've learned to ignore it and not let it bother me. It is what it is in this world. The same people who say these things also show up at our doorstep the next week after fighting with their wives so, it's hard to take them seriously. As I walk down the street, I can hear the faint noise of a slurred argument ending with the smash of a bottle and a man leaving the bar with his hand to his head, blood slowly dripping down his face. We make eye contact momentarily and he scoffs "bitch" under his breath and turns to walk in the other direction. Fine, I wasn't going to show you any sympathy anyway.

As I approach the block the upgrade shop is on, I notice someone standing at the corner with a handful of flyers. They look out of place, nervous as if this was their first time in this part of town. Human, definitely. A flurry of wind brushes past causing the flyers they are holding to go everywhere, one landing near my feet. I briefly scan over the flyer; it details an all-inclusive café opening soon. They're looking for employees.

I decide to help pick up some of the loose flyers as it seems like they desperately need the help. Currently, they are franticly chasing them up and down the street. Quite hilariously, they almost trip over themselves. As I get closer, I seem to notice that this person doesn't look particularly male or female. Could they be like me? They have short black hair that juts out in different directions. They are fairly short and wearing a pair of light-wash overalls with a sunflower tee-shirt underneath.

After I finish picking up the rest of the flyers, I approach them, tapping them on the shoulder. They are startled by my sudden approach and turn quickly to face me.

"Hey, here's the rest of your flyers," I say.

"*Ohmygosh,* thank you so much!" they respond, fidgeting a little bit, not quite sure what to do with all the papers I just handed them. "I started to panic a bit there." Yeah, I could tell.

"It's all good no worries," I start to twist one of the rings I'm wearing as I ask, "What's the deal with the café?"

"Oh, that! It's real neat. A friend and I are trying to start a café where everyone's welcome," they smile as they tell me all about it. "It'll be a place for humans and AIs of any gender identity or sexual orientation to relax... a safe place."

"I've never heard of anything like that, definitely not in New Astartania."

"That's why we're starting it," they pause momentarily, swaying in their place. They kindly extend out one of the flyers to me, "You should check it out."

"Yeah. Yeah, maybe I will," I say with a slight smile and a hint of disbelief. Is there really a chance I can work there? And be accepted as me?

To not have to pretend anymore.

Scorpions
DOMINIKA PETRASOVA

I don't know what I am. I don't know who I am. At least I didn't until today. The truth would've horrified me if I could feel.

Human soldiers, hidden behind the iron shells of their robotic bodies, patrolled the streets. Their synchronous stomping against the broken gravel, sounded like overhead bangs of thunder. My daily alarm. With a single snap of my fingers, the studio flat lit up. Everything was dyed in the steel blue glow of the interactive wallpaper.

I walked over to the red velvet box sitting on the levitating table top beside the bed. Inside was my badge. Carefully, I picked up the black scorpion. Its eyes flashed a crimson red and a prolonged hiss came out of it. It wasn't real, just an imitation.

I pressed it to my upper arm and waited for it to pierce its claws, legs and tail into my skin. The pain was excruciating. It sank deeper into my arm, sending an electric shock down my spine making me drop to my knees. But I knew it'd be over fairly quickly. The scorpion took a moment or two to reconnect to my nervous system.

I turned for the door and from the corner of my eye caught my passing reflection. My hair draped down to my shoulders in stiff curls. The look on my face was frozen in a reflective stare, and a few faint lines crumpled the skin of my forehead.

Outside, I opened an umbrella and started down the street. A street of obsidian houses in the shape of tall rectangles standing on their heads. Numbers marked one half of the front of these houses but there were no fences. No fences were needed. It was practically impossible to breach the neighbouring house and so no burglaries or vandalisms have been reported in almost two decades. The lawns were sensor triggered and, just like the scorpions on everyone's shoulders, the houses too were connected to their owner, recognising or rejecting their gait upon arrival.

At the end of the street I turned and walked some more until I arrived at the police station. A building whose walls were also obsidian but its shape resembled an irregular diamond perched on its tip. I wondered everyday how it remained balanced. At the front door, the scanner light blinded me momentarily. It beeped and the glass doors slid open.

"What a lovely morning, Grace," said the soulless receptionist with the never fading expression of happiness. Even though she was a machine, the smile seemed to drain power out of her.

I waved a customary hand. "Yes, it's alright." I signed in and headed to my office where I grabbed my other badge and attached it to the waist of my slacks. A note sat on the table.

Do me a favour and check out West Avenue. Citizen reported a suspicious looking hearse. – D

Typical Derrick, always leaving the minor crimes up to me. I grabbed my own work car and headed over to West Avenue which was only a few streets away. It was empty and as still as if all of the triangular houses were unoccupied. Everyone was probably at work. I patrolled the street there and back, twice, and found no sign of this mysterious hearse. Deciding that it was most likely a hoax, I tapped on the scorpion badge whose shell lit up. My finger was an inch from calling it in, when I spotted it.

It drifted up the street, leaving a trail of white clouds behind it. I hurried back to my car and, once inside, pressed the cam-

71

ouflage button. No one apart from another police officer was able to see the car once it was cloaked.

I sat there, leaning over the steering wheel, my eyes trained on the shining black hearse as it pulled up a few feet from me. The passenger, a tall and svelte woman, whose face was obscured by a black mask, exited the car while the driver remained inside. She walked to the back and opened the trunk. Inside were dead bodies wrapped up in cling foil. Blood stained the inside and the foil squashed the individual faces, while both ends were tied up in knots. They looked like human larvae.

I tapped a few times on the scorpion on my arm, sending a coded message to the police station. It was against rules and regulations for an officer to intervene alone. In my moment of distraction, the driver must've slipped out of the car because when I looked up again, the driver, a masked man, appeared from behind one of the triangular houses. From house number oh-eleven. He carried a body across his shoulder. The person kicked and squealed, her pale face looked up suddenly and met my eyes. It startled me. No ordinary citizen should've seen me.

That was when I realised it wasn't an ordinary citizen, the being was an older generation human. She didn't have a scorpion badge implemented into her shoulder like its two assailants. The man set the female human down. His partner passed him what looked like a guitar string and he wrapped it around the human's neck, and then yanked. Blood squirted out in every direction and I squinted, despite the fact that none of the blood got onto the windshield of my car. The man enveloped the dead body in fresh cling foil and chucked it on top of the growing pile.

The woman crossed the road and seemed to tap on empty air. But then, the veil disappeared and another, this time white hearse, faded into view. Another masked individual walked out and hauled something heavy onto the floor. Seconds later, the same copy of the female human they had just killed, walked out across the street and strolled into house oh-eleven. By then I was leaning so close that my nose was pressed against the windshield. I noticed that the copy of a human had two red dots shining through the bulge beneath the sleeve of her upper arm. The scorpion.

I fell back into the seat and tried to process what I had just seen. Had those people abducted my human copy too?

The Egyptologist
NADIA REBELO

My watch reads 9:09pm as I pack the last of my things, ready to call it a night when someone slides into the seat opposite me.

'Hello professor.' I look up to find my student Ben laying out some books onto the mahogany surface of the table.

'Ah hello, cramming in late, are we?' I tilt my head to read a title.

'Just some stuff on Egyptology Sir.'

'You're preparing for next semester I see.' I take off my glasses and preoccupy myself with packing the rest of my things away, eager to leave. There is nothing more awkward than interacting with students after office hours.

'Not exactly, I don't know if you saw but they have found a Pyramid on the moon!' I pause my packing.

'Ah yes, they think they have found one due to some images. Who knows what's up there.'

'Well, it's no coincidence.' I look up to find Ben smiling.

'It can be easy to get excited about these things Ben, but until they find some evidence we will never really know.'

'We haven't been back to the moon since like, the 70s. Don't you think that's a little strange?'

'Not really.' I clench my jaw and force a smile.

'What if we haven't been back because they found a bunch of anomalies like the pyramid that point to signs of extra-terrestrial life.'

'You kids and your imagination.' I try to laugh it off but Ben stops smiling.

'Well, I don't suppose you think the Egyptian pyramids were built by humans?'

'Of course, I do.' I snap my briefcase shut and lean back in my chair.

'How would a bunch of humans all the way back then constructed the Pyramids, let alone without any help.'

'Well Ben, those *bunch of humans* happened to be slaves, they spent a lot of time working on those pyramids.'

'I don't buy it.'

'And why is that?'

'Think about it, the pyramids are built of limestone, right? Wasn't there also gold on the tips of the pyramids? Why else would the Pyramids need to be conductive if they were just a bunch of tombs. They are empty after all.'

'Even though the materials are conductive, they hardly work to make up a functioning circuit. As for them being empty, Pyramids were full of wealth, looting was both common and easy. I'm going to need more convincing than that.' I fold my arms.

'How about the fact that the coordinates of the pyramids resemble the speed of light?'

'Oh God, you're a conspirator.' I laugh and shift in my seat.

'Well, isn't it true?'

'Even if it was true, I hardly believe that aliens would have the same units for the speed of light.'

'How would the ancient Egyptians have it? The astronomical configuration of the pyramids aligns with the stars in Orion's belt!' Ben exclaims.

'You do spend a lot of time on Google don't you.' I force another laugh. 'If you want to pass my class I suggest you spend more time reading those books on Egyptology,' I nod towards the books, 'than online conspiracies.'

'Okay Sir, how about this? The ancient Egyptians have a wealth of knowledge, for example the eye of Horus fits perfectly into our brains and the iris of the pupil of the eye represents the pineal gland AKA the-'

I cut him off. 'The third eye, yes I've heard.'

'How would they have *known* that? The eye split into six represents our six senses and aligns within our brain where like, you know what I mean. Where those senses are controlled in the brain.' I genuinely laugh at his struggle to form his argument. 'Seriously, how is it possible for humans to make those pyramids at the speed they did.'

'Alright, are you ready for an exclusive of my class?' I ask leaning forward. Ben nods eagerly. 'Imagine this, you have thousands of slaves working twenty four seven despite the conditions, to build these Pyramids. So, the stones used to build the Pyramids are what? Two tons each? The river Nile is about five miles away from the Pyramids now however, back then the Egyptians would have been more resourceful and created canals and ports to transport these materials. When on land the Egyptians would have used sleds to transport the rocks, wetting the sand in front of them enabling the sleds to move easily, well, as easily as they can. In fact, there have been wall paintings discovered that depict this which were mistaken for a purifying ceremony in the past. They would have had a number of people pulling these sleds I'm sure.' Ben nodded leaning forward taking in all of the information that I was spoon-feeding him.

'Now, as for their knowledge for example of the stars, the ancient Egyptians were very intelligent people. They would have spent years studying the constellations, constructing the Pyramids, they had a wealth of information. They were well beyond their years, advanced beings but that is purely down to time and intelligence.'

'I guess,' Ben replied but I could tell he needed more convincing.

'Now, to say that aliens gave Egyptians their knowledge and built their pyramids, we are disregarding huge accomplishments from people of colour. You must be careful when speaking about these things because it can be very offensive, do you understand what I'm saying?'

Ben is frowning and I assume he is mirroring my own features so I try my best to relax my face. 'I guess I never really thought of it like that, have I offended you?'

I smile and let out a breath I didn't realise that I was holding. 'No of course not, I understand that these things can be interesting and exciting to say the least. It's important to realise that we are in a very privileged position, sitting where we are today. We live in a country built off of colonialism, stolen culture, artefacts, you name it. Speculating like this can contribute to the erasure of culture and history for people of colour.'

'I completely understand, you have completely opened my eyes, thank you Sir, I look forward to starting your class.'

'Good lad, read up on those books, they will be most beneficial for my course.' I gather my things and get up.

'Thanks for the talk professor.' Ben smiles up at me and begins to open his books.

'My pleasure, it was a very fascinating conversation.' Ben nods and I begin to walk away.

I rush out of the library and into the streets of London, the rain spattering lightly on my skin. I let it soothe me as I walk down a dank alleyway, rummaging around my blazer pocket for my phone.

'Stupid fucking humans.' I murmur under my breath as I call my associate at S4. They were on to us.

Gone Phishin'
KASEY SMITH

"**W**hat'd you find, little phisherman?" said Zaykho as he reclined in the chair, lighting the blunt of synthetic cannabis that hung between his lips.

"This." Toke turned his monitor toward Zaykho.

Zaykho leant forward through the cloud of smoke settled around his head. Toke scrolled through page after page of design schematics - line drawings, proof of concept models, and complex mathematical equations.

"The fuck is it?" Zaykho's voice was made deeper by the smoke.

"Blueprints," Toke turned the monitor back towards himself, "For a new gene-editing augment designed to decrease the chance of user DNA corruption."

Zaykho let out a barking laugh that made Toke jump.

"Very nice, phisherman," Zaykho passed the blunt with a crooked smile. "Big catch. Who got tangled in ya net?"

Toke held the blunt awkwardly between his forefinger and thumb as he smoked.

"Some low level *TwoFourtyFive* intern," Toke coughed as he spoke, "Dickhead gave me full access to his work account. I was quick - smash and grab, init. By the time they booted me, I'd already cloned everything. Wasn't much else worth shit on there

79

though. Personal data, account numbers and that. Pennies in comparison."

"Okay, okay. I see you." Zaykho stood, made even taller inside the small room, "I'll ask around, set up the buy."

Toke held out a USB drive.

"Thirty thousand. Nothing less." Toke pulled the USB away from Zaykho's reaching hand. "Fifty-fifty cut, yeah?"

Zaykho's lips curled back into a smile revealing teeth plated with tarnished silver.

"Say nothing, phisherman. No less, no more. Equal partners?" They shook hands. Toke gave Zaykho the drive. "Alright, in a bit."

Zaykho killed the car's engine but left the headlights on - two beams cutting through the pitch black. Before stepping out, he adjusted the sawn-off pushed into the waistband of his jeans.

Off the dirt road, Zaykho could see Schwartz leaning against the hood of his prized mustang. He was unnaturally large. A body sculpted by testosterone therapy and silicone implants. Zaykho thought it was fucking embarassing to play pretend like that, but Schwartz was his only option for offloading gene-mods.

Zaykho stopped a few metres from the mustang. "What you saying, Schwartz? You good?"

"Why not light off a flare?" Schwartz nodded at Zaykho's car, his voice a mix of native English and a forced, vaguely Eastern-European accent.

"I weren't the one who wanted to meet outside the city. Can't see in the dark." Zaykho laughed.

"Shut the fuck up," Schwartz pushed off the car and walked forward, "You're always so fucking loud."

Schwartz watched Zaykho, flexing his implants and grinding his jaw. Zaykho could see the testosterone coursing through the muscle-freak, could feel the animal aggression building, and remembered the shotgun pressed against his thigh.

"Relax." Zaykho took a step back and pulled the small USB from his pocket. "Here."

Schwartz untensed. He turned and waved at the mustang and the passenger door popped open. A small man stepped out. Zaykho almost laughed at the image of the two of them crammed side by side into the mustang. The small man carried a laptop that he placed on the hood of Schwartz's car before turning to Zaykho with his hand out.

"Give him the stick." Schwartz puffed up his chest.

Zaykho threw the USB past Schwartz to the little man by the car.

"Now fuck off." Schwartz stepped forward, bloated arms crossed across his swollen chest.

"Pay me." Zaykho stood his ground.

"You get paid when we sell it." Schwartz spat the words onto Zaykho's face. "Now leave, unless you wanna swallow those stupid fucking silver teeth." Zaykho smiled, let out a small laugh and wiped his face. If that's how Schwartz wanted to do business, Zaykho thought.

"You got a buyer?" asked Zaykho.

"What?" Schwartz's accent slipped a little. "None of your fucking business."

"Does he know who the buyer is?" Zaykho nodded at the little man by the car, who'd stopped looking at the laptop and was anxiously watching.

Schwartz twisted his thick neck to glance over at his associate, then looked back at Zaykho. There was a moment of silence. Zaykho watched the veins in Schwartz's head swell, and listened to his breathing quicken. Tell tale signs, but Schwartz probably didn't even notice. Self-awareness had never been Schwartz's forte. Zaykho pressed his hand against the shotgun grip beneath his t-shirt, waiting.

It happened quickly. Schwartz lunged forward, his swollen hands reaching for Zaykho's neck. He was agile - silicone is lighter than muscle - but Zaykho had seen it coming. In one fluid motion, Zaykho lopped back, limbs like liquid, drew the shotgun and unloaded both barrels point blank into Schwartz chest. When Schwartz hit the dirt, there was still a misted cloud of blood and silicone hanging in the cool night's air. Zaykho stepped over the mountainous corpse and approached the little man standing frozen by the mustang.

"Now," Zaykho loaded two shells into the shotgun and snapped it closed, "Tell me about this buyer."

It was the lunch rush and the diner was crowded.

Zaykho stepped inside and looked around. He saw the buyer sitting by himself in a booth near the back.

"You Carlisle?" Zaykho slid into the booth.

"Where's Schwartz?" Carlisle wiped his mouth with a paper napkin then dropped it on his plate.

"Schwartz is out of business, but I'm not." Zaykho rested one arm on the table, the other against his stomach and smiled.

"And who the fuck are you?" Carlisle almost sounded polite.

"Zaykho. Here" Zaykho slid the USB across the table. Carlisle took it and put it in the breast pocket of his coat. From another pocket Carlisle pulled out a credit chip. Zaykho tapped it against his RFID scanner.

"We agreed thirty thousand." Zaykho ran his tongue across his teeth, jaw clenched.

"You killed my supplier. Consider it reparations, a gesture of goodwill from you to me." said Carlisle.

Zaykho carefully drew the shotgun and rested it on Carlisle's knee below the table. The barrel pressed against his stomach. Carlisle just smiled, nodded at something behind Zaykho. He turned. Every single person in the diner was watching him. Their hands buried in waistbands or under shirts. Zaykho looked from face to face, then withdrew the shotgun and placed it on the seat beside him. Almost immediately the diners resumed what they'd been doing: eating and making small talk as if nothing had happened.

"If you want to make money, real money, then leave the street tactics at home. If you find anything else, call me. Now take the twenty thousand and fuck off." Carlisle spoke to the back of Zaykho's head, who was still watching the people in the diner in disbelief.

Slowly, Zaykho took the credit chip off the table, stood with wounded pride and skulked out of the diner with less money than he'd promised Toke he'd get.

About the author:

Kasey Smith is an aspiring novelist born and raised in Hayes, North-West London. He studies creative writing at Brunel University. Kasey uses his writing to reflect on his past, and escape into the future.

A Wild Witch In America
NATASHA STEWART

The warrior witches of a desert town walk along the horizon, patrolling along sand dunes and tumbledown cattle ranches at sunset. The moon rises, but they don't see it– magic, hearing, taste serves as their eyes– for there are only a few stars left above the wild west. The night is watching...until a moment, twilight, can become a beast once more.

Midnight awakens; stars explode around your battalion, who quickly draw their rifles to load spells into the barrel. Everyone looks up. Two eyes blink in the ashes of a crumbing constellation, which allows the night to push them apart to grow teeth. This wild west isn't normal. Magic made the night *hungry*. A day later, the bodies of the witches are spat out, like fish bones, across the town square. Monti, walking out of the salon, drink in hand, chokes when seeing you – her sister – among them.

"Don't get smart with me –" A leaflet was flapped in front of Monti's face by her mother, two days after the attack. "The brigade is for witches like her; not witches like you,"

The leaflet was small. 'Recruitment' in big red letters.

"What do you mean like me?"

"For sorcery's sake, witches like your sister! People who don't drink and shit their pants when anyone tries to defeat that thing!"

Silence.

"Montgomery. I didn't –"

"I am going...whether you like it or not." Monti sighed and placed a pointed hat and glinting revolver on the table. It was standard equipment. In the several hours she spent verifying her sister's body, she had signed up to patrol the border, as a witch turned soldier.

"Do you want to end up like her?"

After a second, Monti answered her mother.

"She always wanted me to change."

Whether it was karma or a dare between recruits, change came in the form of a spell: one that whipped past Monti's face to pierce a barn door. A smoking hole appeared above Monti's head, making everyone turn around to where she had been hiding and avoiding....

"Jonesy! How many fucking times—get some glasses or pay attention!"

Attention. Several weeks had passed since Monti left home, to join the battalion. Their 'battlement' was a crumbling cattle range, where a horde of young girls were often clumped together like cattle and not witches turned soldiers. Monti mainly focused on blending in and was successful for a while, until that misfired spell resulted in a blonde woman, wearing a captain's uniform, walking forward.

"Just a scratch, luckily," She was tall, like Monti. But as where she had spent most of her life as a twig, the captain was the whole damn tree. "Unlike bullets, spells don't always shoot straight—"

Suddenly, she stopped. Her eyes pinched together, and parchments appeared in her hand, with a click. Monti's name was written in red – circled twice.

"You're Monti, aren't you?" The captain kissed her teeth. "Several complaints from instructors... you refused marksmanship training? "

Monti shook her head.

"No – as in you didn't refuse or refused to do it?"

Monti shrugged, awkwardly. A pistol was then chucked towards her, drawn from the captain's thigh holster with a laugh. Monti didn't move for what felt like several minutes. Her chest was tight. The captain walked up. Monti was shoved back – hard – into haystacks. Everybody was watching.

"You're afraid. How sweet..."

The barrel of the gun rose, like the hand of a clock. It landed inches away from the captain's forehead.

"Coward." She spat. "Shoot. Do it! What are you waiting for? Shoot—"

Bang!

Bang! Bang! Ban—

An explosion turned into a jet of red-hot flames. The captain had seconds to duck, as the fire exploded above her and sank into the barn's wooden walls. Incantations sucked up the smoke and flames afterwards, revealing...daylight. A familiar small hole had turned into an absent wall.

"My name is Captain Goodie," The captain said, smiling "How do you feel about patrolling?"

◆ ◆ ◆

The offer was unpredicted. Dangerous.

She would have to be brave, if she took the offer to patrol the border early, without the normal six months of training. Monti believed that she couldn't rise to the challenge, so she rejected the offer...initially. Weeks flew by, calmly, side to side with Goodie. The captain made her read, learn through tracing ley line maps and grimoires. Goodie's words of encouragement allowed her confidence to bloom, and Monti soon rose through the ranks. But the fear didn't leave. Bodies do...when Monti finally gave into Goodie's pushing.

"You're drunk,"

"No shit!" Monti replied, sitting on the barn roof. A few bottles crashed below. "I'm as drunk as tailor— sailor...fuck it."

"Monti," Goodie said.

"I wasn't ready to patrol. I told you... and you still fucking forced me!" Another bottle crashed. "I got people killed!"

One moment. One second, where she felt like being brave had turned into a disaster. When she had chased the beast — leaving her section of the battalion unguarded — weak.

All that was left behind was several crushed heads, grains of bone among the sand. Monti turned to face her mentor.

"I'm a coward. I run. That's what I do." She continued. "Why are we even trying? It's going to kill us anyway."

"You haven't been paying attention, have you?" Goodie stood up. "It was never about being brave or a soldier–"

Monti scoffed and turned her back. Goodie sighed.

"I have patrol again. I'll see you tomorrow,"

Tomorrow never came for Goodie.

The idiots Monti put in charge, and it was all wrong. Like a sheep in wolf's clothing, her mind practically screamed 'imposter', as every witch looked to her for guidance. Hope. It's only when another girl burns a hole in a wall that she finds herself saying–

"Holy magic. You know nothing at all,"

So, she taught. They learned and life surprisingly got easier. One night, she even laughed, as a couple of recruits magicked a spotlight and created shadow puppets. During the merriment, one of the lower captains taped her on the shoulder and whispered that she was needed on patrol. Monti followed, learning what her mentor was trying to teach. It was never about bravery or being a good soldier. It was about the effort to try and make a difference.

The night grew and ripped apart witches' limbs like confetti, pushing Monti through the open air. She flung spell after spell; one after another, bursting like the stars long before. She became numb, bleeding out on the sand.

At least Monti can call herself a real Witch.

About the author:

Natasha Stewart is a South London writer studying in Uxbridge. Her writing has been featured in The Brunel Draft and a previous anthology, which was named 'Tall Tales & Rapid Rhymes'. She is currently studying Creative Writing at Brunel University and hopes to take a PHD in English Literature. She wants to publish more poetry and short stories in the future, exploring possible blends between history, fantasy, and our sense of self.

Chronophobia
H.C. WHITE

I remember the first time I ever truly listened to my father's words was the same day that his voice fell silent. I was only nine when he died. He had loved to talk, but seldom had much to say, I thought, and so I had spent much of the time humouring him. Hearing him, but not really listening. Then, suddenly, on that day, all he had ever said, all at once, came echoing through the chambers of my mind like a battle cry.

My childhood was largely uneventful before then. My parents had remained together, we had remained in the home I was born in, and I had never needed to move school. I did not have many friends, but the ones I did have were kind and sincere. We were neither well-off, nor dirt-poor. I had some of the latest toys, but not many. Summers felt long, Christmases special, and I knew in my heart that everything would always feel like this. Nothing would ever change.

Despite my certainty of the perpetuity of our comfort, my father, in all his misguided cynicism, was unconvinced. He would often smile down at me, playing, or practising the piano, or laughing at a book I was reading, and then rub my hair. The smile he wore would give way to eyes which seemed drowned in bittersweet sentiment, and he would say:

"Cherish these times, my son. They go by so quickly. Time just seems to disappear from you when you're my age."

Honestly, I had no idea what he was talking about. I had been alive forever, and I had never changed. Neither had he. Nothing ever changed, Dad. He was silly like that. I thought that perhaps he just watched too many movies, or maybe he'd hit his head too hard.

"Relax," I thought to myself. "You're worrying for nothing."

Then came the day when I found a body in the kitchen; a cold pile of flesh and vomit which I swear looked just like him. It had his hair, his scared eyes, and it even wore his wedding ring on the hand which clung at his chest, but it wasn't him. The sun hadn't even risen yet, and I had come down, dreary-eyed, to get some blackcurrant juice because I'd woken up thirsty. When I saw it lying there, I assumed I must be dreaming, so I didn't say anything. I didn't feel scared, either. I just stood there, staring at it, waiting to wake up.

The room lay perfectly still for a while, whilst I stared at the dad-shaped vision, and the dad-shaped vision stared right back at me. It didn't blink. Just stared. The low hum of the fridge against which the vision's head weighed was the only thing to be heard.

I looked down again at the dad-shaped creature, which still hadn't moved, and wondered why I hadn't yet woken up. This was a boring dream. Then, I heard footsteps from the stairs. They were Mum's. I could always tell if it was Mum or Dad coming just by listening to their footsteps. I didn't turn to see her arrive, but I knew she was here when I heard her scream like I'd never heard anyone scream before. I turned around and she had fallen to her knees and was screaming and crying and crying and screaming, and I really, really wanted to wake up at this point. I focused hard through her screams to listen to the stairs and wondered why I couldn't hear Dad's footsteps thundering down them. His were much heavier than hers. I would have heard them. He's a heavy sleeper, but not *that* heavy.

Mum crawled forward on her hands and knees in a way that looked just like my little sister. She was just under a year old, and her arms would flail out as she tried to move forward. It was really funny to watch. Somehow, I didn't think mum was trying to be funny. She grabbed the dad-shaped thing by the collar of its shirt and shook really hard, kind of like how Dad does when we play 'electric shock.' She did this a few times, but nothing happened. She must have run out of energy from shaking so hard because she went all limp and fell on its chest and went really quiet, her face buried down into its body. Her hand crawled about on it like a spider until she found its hand, and she held it really tight. She squeezed it over and over, but it didn't squeeze back.

Me, my Mum, and the body were alone in silence for a while, until all of the sudden that quiet was devastated by the ticking of a clock. A really loud one. It ticked once and once only, but it reverberated with such gravitas around the room that I felt I could almost see the soundwaves. In fact, I could feel them, like pulses of adrenaline that flushed through my body. Perhaps we were inside the unseen clock. I looked back to my mum, who didn't seem to have heard it, and the thing she was sitting on, and she opened her arms and begged me to come and give her a hug, so I did, and the moment I did I started crying as hard as my mum. I didn't even know why, I just felt like there was nothing else that I could have done.

The next time I heard the tick was at his funeral a few weeks later. Mum had explained it to me then, and I just remember thinking this was the longest dream I'd ever had, and I was getting really annoyed. They left the casket open and the tick came the moment I saw his face. It was so loud that it made me jump and I worried that I'd accidentally slammed the coffin shut. Mum made me say goodbye, even though I didn't want to.

The tick came back more and more frequently after that. Now I hear it almost every day, sometimes more than once. It seems, really, to be speeding up. It never gets any quieter, though. Every time I hear it, I still get that little adrenaline rush and it scares the shit out of me. It can take me hours to recover. I am grateful, at least, that it reminds me to tell my boy, who's twelve

91

now, and full of innocent wonder and joy:

"Cherish these times, my son. They go by so quickly."

About the author:

H.C. White is a young writer, musician, and theatre-maker from London who grew up in a working-class, east-end family, and fell into the creative arts largely by accident. His work often deals with the existential and the ephemeral and tries to articulate the bittersweet beauty of the human condition. He often thinks lyrically and music-ally in his word and phrase choices, often playfully exploiting rhythm and rhyme.

How Captain Rex Lost His Eye
WILL WITHAM

So there I was; staring out amongst the ocean grey. Not blue, very much grey. The mist was thick, thicker than it had been in months. Clouds almost as black as charcoal blotted out the sun, leaving us alone in this dark world. Our vision was so obscured, you couldn't even see your own reflection in the water.

The Upchungle was plodding along, she looked much better back in those days mind you, and her sails were finding what little wind was around as she pulled us through the fog. Now, me crew were all greenies and you could tell by their sea legs. They were tryna follow me orders but it got to the point where almost all of 'em were filling the ocean with their breakfasts. This left me, standing at the helm alone, and steering best I could.

Something was wrong. In this world, you don't get random fogs this thick. No. Someone, or something, was out there. Me eyes pierced through the haze like lightning. Me scales, while still the dull bronze they are now, were shining in the dark; I was a beacon back in the day. A symbol of hope and leadership. It was in moments like these that me crew (me old crew that is) would look to me and obey my every order. Not these though. Maybe I pushed 'em too hard, but the sea isn't a lady for the weak of heart and stomach.

The Defender, me trusty greataxe, was in me left hand while I steered with me right. The hat I wear now was balanced on me head. The only thing that separates me now from me younger self is missing me eye and much more back pain. But if you ask me, a little bit of lumbago and only one good eye is more than a fair payout for experience.

We had been in the fog for maybe four hours when The Upchungle hit something. Something big.

'I think we hit a rock, Captain.' Young Benjamin called to me between wretches. Foolish boy. I couldn't blame the kid too much, he'd not had the chance to feel the difference. To understand the noise changes of us hitting something and something hitting us.

'Get away from the sides, lads!' The boys ran to me shakily, their bodies still not used to the waves. The Upchungle had fully stopped in the water now, simply rocking to the ocean's push.

I grabbed The Defender and braced meself. Alistair, the youngest member, slowly edged to the side of the ship and peered over. Damn fool. We couldn't see what did it, but his body fell to the floor with a sickening 'thunk' and began to leak blood from the stump on his neck. Immediately, the other 'sailors' began screaming. I told 'em to shut their yaps but they continued. The terror in each other's voices was the last thing most of 'em heard.

Rising ominously from the deep, a silhouette was cast upon the sheet of fog. Instinctively, I let loose a stream of lightning from me mouth right into the shadow. We watched the shadow avoid me attack with superb reflexes, I was almost impressed.

Apparently me breath attack was the final push on the weather as it began to rain. I tell you boys, this is rain like you'd never seen before. The raindrops were cannonballs, exploding on the deck of The Upchungle and filling the rim of me hat. Glaring into the fog, I watched as lightning illuminated the backdrop of me foe.

Suddenly one of the crew, I think his name was Travis but we all called him Jonesy, screamed and ran towards the shadow. His voice was filled with determination and purpose. He would've made a fine sailor.

Jonesy darted towards the being and leapt upon the side of the ship. As he pushed off the ground, he slipped in the rain and his shins smashed into the side of The Upchungle. We watched as Jonesy tumbled over the side of the ship and the beastie revealed itself.

Five heads moved from the mist. Their faces were serpent-like but each had a different eye colour. Moving independently of each other, they ripped apart Jonesy in front of us, tasting his flesh and not stopping to savour him. The hydra stared at us. Its nostrils flared as it sniffed the air before letting out a blood wrenching screech. I'm not sure if you boys have ever heard a dragon's roar but multiply it by five and that's what this sounded like.

The lads, of course, lost 'emselves and began crying and screaming. Couldn't blame 'em, but it sure didn't help the situation. Snapping at the ones that ran and devouring their flesh, the hydra tore through most of me crew in seconds. The only ones left was meself and Young Benjamin.

Grasping the boy by his arm, I told him 'Listen 'ere, boy. I'm gonna go kill this thing, I want you to take The Upchungle and get 'er moving again, you 'ear me?'. It took the boy a moment before he nodded and ran to the helm.

Swinging up The Defender into both me hands, I charged the beast. Adrenaline was filling me body, you understand, and I was feeling that familiar sense of purpose and destiny coursing through me veins and soul. I slashed through two of the heads in one fell swoop. The partial carcasses flopped onto the deck before me as I grinned at the dreadful terror. Foolish of me to not remember what a hydra is known for. Of course four more heads grew back in seconds. Bone cracking, flesh stretching, blood bubbling. Due to my dragon heritage, I am incapable of vomiting but the noise alone nearly made me throw up me whiskey. I shan't be forgetting that again.

The hydra darted it's heads at me. I dodged and dipped and dived (remember I had no back pain then), narrowly surviving their volley of attacks. Snarling at the beast, I stood up on the side of The Upchungle and did the unthinkable… apart from when Jonesy tried it; I jumped off. The only difference between Jonesy and I, I'm still here!

I barged me way past their bulbous necks and landed on its back. Burying The Defender deep into the hydra's back, carving deep gashes into it. Fun fact I learned that day: a hydra can't turn its head very well. I stood upon its hide, ripping into it over and over again, until, eventually, it fell back into the ocean.

I, Captain Rexminster, had slain the mighty hydra.

Hmm? How did I lose me eye? Oh right! Well I was climbing back aboard The Upchungle and apparently there was an exposed nail. Bloody 'urt, I tell you that.

BOOKS IN THIS SERIES

*Brunel University London
Anthologies*

More Horror, Sci-fi & Fantasy flash fiction by Creative Writing students:

Faeries, Fiends & Flying Saucers

Wizards, Werewolves & Weird Engines

Robots, Rogues & Revenants

FOLLOW BRUNEL
CREATIVE WRITING:

Blog https://brunelwriter.com/
Instagram /brunelwriter
Twitter @BrunelWriter
Facebook /BrunelWriter

Printed in Great Britain
by Amazon

80876250R00062